Entity
The Complete Trilogy!

M. Purkiss

Copyright © 2024 M. Purkiss

All characters and locations in this book are completely fictional. Any resemblance to real people or places are completely coincidental and unintentional.

1

All rights reserved.

Cover image created by Ashley's Photography.

ISBN: 9798320985275
Imprint: Independently published

SPECIAL THANKS AND DEDICATIONS

To all my family, friends and readers who have supported me since the beginning. This complete Entity trilogy marks a new era in my writing journey. I hope you will all stick around for the next chapter!

Thanks to all for helping me create this book!

ENTITY

Prologue

The air was mild and the sound of crickets could be heard coming from the fields and meadows surrounding the English town, Merryville. It was quiet and picturesque, the hills were a perfect shade of green. The setting looked like something from a postcard, it was faultless. It was a pleasant place to live, not many people lived here. Sunny days brought people out and about. Reading in the park, walking around leisurely admiring the stunning countryside. Children would play in the forest and fields. Simple fun, something seen less these days. Many children play on their devices and spend endless hours on game consoles. It made some parents worry that the future might be talking to a machine all day, rather than interacting with people. Many happy memories were made in Merryville, much like any other town in the world. The residents would watch out for each other.

    Merryville had very few shops, but the ones they did have seemed busy most of the time. There was a general store, as well as a fish and chip shop and car parts outlet, among other businesses. The town also had one local public house which was called 'The Hill's Angel', named so because it is situated on a high part of town, overlooking the lush scenery.

The sun was beginning to set on the town after another perfect summer's day. Everyone who worked, now travelling home to be with their loved ones. There wasn't a cloud in the sky and the evening was warm.

One of the families enjoying the seemingly perfect evening was the Petersons. The head of the household, George Peterson and his wife Jane, along with their only child James, lived in a cozy country house. A house built with love, it had a thatched roof, old fashioned brick work and century old architecture. It was not the most spectacular of houses, but for the Petersons it was home.

George was a simple farmer who sold his produce to the local stores and out of town grocers, he would work all day to meet his deadlines. He always had worked hard to put the food on the table, even harder when times were tough. He would always be up early to tend to his produce and be home late to be sure he had done all his jobs. Within Merryville, he was a very popular man, he had many friends and even more acquaintances. He would always be seen wearing his welly boots and his tweed suit. His hair always seemed to have a scruffy look to it, now greying with age and dusty from the days of labor. He had the most brilliant blue eyes, piercing. His family was the most important thing in the world for him. All he had were the two of them, he was an only child and his parents died when he was just making his transition into adulthood. He could not remember a time before or after where he felt so much pain, physically and emotionally. He met Jane shortly after and the two immediately "clicked" and they soon swore to be with each other till the end of their days.

Jane, was a receptionist at the local doctors surgery, her job involved mundane tasks; answering the telephone, making appointments, making sure that everyone had coffee. The lackey of the surgery really, she didn't mind though. She had brilliantly bright blond hair with loose curls. She always wore red lipstick, but not much else in terms of make up. She was a natural beauty. She, like George, had been an only child, both her parents died when she was pregnant with James. Her dad to bowel cancer and her mum died in a horrific car accident. She had been so close to her parents and she had found it difficult to come to terms with. They both had fairly tragic lives, they bonded with each other over them.

They had each other's shoulder to cry on.

Their son, James, was in secondary school, nearly there, nearly finished. Just his final exams to go then off to college for young James. He was a small lad for the age of sixteen. He had thin legs and arms. He always donned a bob haircut, the sort of haircut which looked like a home job. He was good in school and always studied. He did not mind school but looked forward to college, to study science, his most beloved subject.

The Petersons had neighbours, who were about a mile away from them. They visited them on a regular basis, for dinner or a chat. As a family they were quite social but they never went out much, Jane would normally volunteer to host parties at their home. Almost everyone in town knew them, many people would regard them even as friends. James did not like the home parties though, he felt obliged to interact with people he didn't much like or in some cases he did not even know. Although for his parents he would grin a bear it.

It was at one of these social parties that something happened. Something which changed the lives of everyone on earth…forever.

Chapter 1

Dear Diary,

    Sorry I haven't wrote in your pages for such a long time. This morning I awoke with a new motivation to revisit you. I had the most peculiar and most real dream I have ever had. I woke this morning with a chief headache, even the lights above me hurt my eyes. I winced back from the morning light as I drew back the curtains. I crawled back into bed and covered my head with the duvet to stop the pain. Obviously the headache was not the reason for this new found motivation, it was the dream.

    I felt like I was so far away, further than I had ever been before. The smell was unusual to my nostrils. I could hear some people talking behind the walls which surrounded me. They were speaking in foreign tongues. I felt so relaxed. The sound of the muffled voices were unnerving but in a way quite soothing. The dream continued on this way for a while. I glanced around the small room in which I lay, but there was no one else occupying the space, Just me. The sound of the muffled voices got a bit louder. They were approaching me, the soothing sensation I felt before, now turned to fear and anxiety.

Suddenly, a bright light appeared before me. Someone opened a door to where I was and I was blinded by the brilliant light outside. As the room was illuminated, I was able to take in my surroundings for very few seconds. I remember, I was laying on a chair of some sort, similar to that of a dentist, maybe slightly different. Before I took in much more the door to the room closed and the room turned gloomy again. I heard a "click" sound come from somewhere and a small light shone from the ceiling above my face. It was just enough light to brighten the room slightly.

My eyes suddenly started to become

blurry. Maybe I was waking up, but the dream held onto me as long as it could. Then I heard someone speak, this time they were speaking in English and I could understand everything they were saying.

'We are losing it,' a low and husky voice said.

'We had better be quick then,' another voice said. The voices sounded very similar. Both were deep and both sounded monotone. My vision faded even further, I was sure that I was going to wake up soon. I could see two figures standing over me, I could not make out their faces though. My vision was too faded.

Just when I thought it was over, the first voice spoke again.

'Doctor, you need to do it now.'

'OK, hold it still.'

There was a sudden rush of pain, like someone literally stabbing me in the head. I could feel my head pumping with every heartbeat I took.

I awoke shortly after in my bed. The headache still screaming to me. The dream *felt so real. It amazes me how the human brain can turn what is happening in a dream and make the feelings real. I remained under the duvet for a good half hour before coming out from under. My head still aches a bit, but the pain has eased a little.*

I am so glad we had this little time to catch up. I hope to write to you more regularly now that I have started again. Until next time,

Your again loyal writer.

It was a warm summer's night in June, the sun still hanging in the sky painted the sky with bright pink and orange. The birds were singing their final verses of the day before they nested for the night and the owl would start its call, signaling the night. There was a warm breeze which drifted over the hills of the countryside. The smell of the air was fresh and clean.

The Petersons were hosting their annual summer BBQ, there was quite a gathering of people and both George and Jane were sure that they did not know all of them. They were not one to make a scene though, they would carry on and serve the food. The more the merrier.

James was occupying himself in his bedroom playing video games and listening to the latest song craze. He hoped no one would miss his absence from the party and had snuck out through the patio doors and up the stairs discreetly. George and Jane didn't notice as it goes, they had been pre occupied with the preparation and cooking of the food. George, as head chef, wore a novelty chef hat with a neon bright pattern on it, a present from Jane for his birthday ready for the summer of BBQs. Jane wore a stunning black skirt and blouse two piece, finished with white diamonds which reflected the perfect sunset shining down.

'I hope you and George can join our party next week,' said their oldest neighbour Mrs. White. She was an elderly woman of eighty-nine and was still on the go all the time, she drove still and attended all the events she could, although her asthma could become scary at times.

'I'm sure we can, Nora. I will telephone you in the week though, just in case,' Jane replied, her mind already searching for an excuse. Nora was a kind natured woman who always had a tight perm and big jewel ear rings, sometimes they didn't match, Nora's eyes are not what they were.

'Well, I will be listening out for that ringing then. Have you seen Wendy? Did I tell you she's going to be going to medical school soon,' she quizzed.

'I think you have mentioned it once or twice. No I haven't seen her in years as it goes,' Jane said. She had heard this story for the past two years and was wondering when Wendy was actually leaving. She didn't want to think that Nora was going round the bend. Possible though.

'I miss her,' Nora said.

'Have you not seen her?' Jane asked but had no reply. She turned to pour some more drinks.

Wendy was Nora's grandchild, fresh out of college and was about to embark on a wonderful life. Jane turned to Nora to talk to her about Wendy some more, but Nora was already telling the same story to someone else.

Saves me the headache, she thought. Jane looked around at the party guests and it filled her with such joy to think that they had so many friends. As she glanced around with a grace unexpected from a farmer's wife, she spotted Mr. and Mrs. Robinson, sipping on some champagne. She moved towards the pair.

'Hello,' she said, reaching out her hand for him, arms open for a hug from her.

'Hi Jane, what a lovely BBQ. We are hoping to host a party soon, to celebrate Bills big promotion,' Lucia said, glancing over at Bill to see if he heard.

'Oh, congratulations Bill. I wish you the best of

luck.' She hugged him.

'Thank you Jane,' he said and embraced her. Jane saw that Lucia was rubbing her head, grimacing in pain it looked like.

'Are you ok, Lucia?' Jane asked.

'Yeah I'm fine. I woke up with a bit of a niggling feeling. It will pass. Probably just the heat getting to me,' she said shaking it off. She smiled again and Jane felt reassured she was OK.

The evening moved at a steady pace, everyone had drinks. Everyone seemed happy, laughing and joking with each other. It was so nice to see so many people from the town being so friendly. It was definitely a party to lead by example.

The smell of the BBQ filled the air.

'Burgers ready,' called George from the grill. As he said that the people stopped what they were doing and swarmed around the BBQ like moths to a flame. This happened at all parties and George learnt to just stand back and let people fight over how well done they liked their burgers.

'You would of thought that they had never eaten before, ha,' George chuckled, walking towards where Jane was standing, looking out over the hills.

'Wonderful night isn't it George?'

'Amazing, absolutely amazing,' he confirmed and looked around. 'Where is James, has he escaped the pleasures of listening to Nora go on about how she changed his nappies as a baby,' He said and they laughed in unison.

'Probably, lucky boy. Just leave him, he will be down when he is hungry,' Jane said.

The sun was nearly out of view and the summer night was creeping in. The sky was free from clouds and other obstructions, apart from a few sparkling stars which hung in the air. The breeze was still warm but cooling down more and more by the second. The sky was still bright pink, but now changing to a dark purple colour. The smell of freshly cooked burgers was everywhere they turned their heads. The birds which were chirping earlier had now nested for the night and the owl occasionally hooted its song. In the distance the sound of crickets was audible, a beautiful sunset fell over the English town which was absolutely stunning on the backdrop of hills, all different shades of greens, like a patchwork quilt. The seemingly endless space which surrounded the Petersons home, made them all feel so free.

'Well, the sausages won't cook themselves,' said George.

'Ok, honey I'll be over in a moment, this scene is just too amazing to walk away from,' she said. He kissed her on the cheek and resumed his position behind the grill. Jane just basked in the glory of the transition from day into night. The sky gradually became darker by the second, which gave way to more amazing colours, purples and blues. It brought a tear to her eye, which slowly trickled down her cheek, a happy tear. As she cast her eyes across the sky, she caught sight of a twinkling star in the distance shining bright, brighter than any other star before. Jane stood for a moment watching it and then turned to face the party again and walked back to join the rest of the guests.

James came down for some food and drinks when the guests began to depart. He spied Nora and tried to avoid her with success, although it was a close call. As he walked down the stairs he misjudged the last step and fell, making a "thud" at the bottom. A few guests looked his way, but the one he was trying to avoid did not. He grabbed a burger and returned to his position upstairs. He stared out of the window in his bedroom and caught a glimpse of a bright star in the sky, James was very interested in the solar system and planets. He would spend hours outside in the cold, wind and hot weather just staring literally into space. Everything about it amazed him. If you think about it, it is a miracle how all the planets communicate with the stars and seasons, James thrived on it. He could tell you information on stars, suns, moons from different planets. His parents always listened with complete interest in what their son was saying, as he himself was interested and enthusiastic about telling them different facts.

This star, there was something about it that seemed very strange. It was not only the brightest star he had seen but it seemed to be growing as well, changing shape in the sky. He watched with fascination for a few minutes. Then he began to see what was happening.

James ran frantically down stairs through the rest of the party guests and pointed their attention to the bright star in the sky. He could not talk at all, he had a face which was petrified. Jane looked up and noticed that it was the same star she had seen but now much bigger, much closer.

'What is it honey?' Jane asked concerned. She thought it was some spectacular solar system event they were witnessing, it was in a way. Then she studied the star a bit more closely. It was moving towards the surface of Earth. The star was not a star, it was bright, but not a star. Everyone looked at it more closely, but no one could see what it actually was that was plummeting towards them. It got closer still, people at the party began to panic and leave. Some were on mobile phones and speaking with loved ones. In a state of panic no one knew what to do. Some people screamed as the impact was sure to be imminent. The object moving towards them got brighter still, they almost had to look away for short times to regain their sight, the way some people might do when looking at the sun. The ground rumbled as the bright light gained on them.

It stopped.

The night was deadly quiet, not a peep from anyone or anything except an owl and some evening crickets. The world seemed to be muted. Uncomfortable, George broke the silence, which seemed to last an age.

'It is probably nothing,' he reassured everyone. No one was convinced of course. They couldn't be just OK with something rapidly coming towards Earth. The star stayed in the sky at the same shape and size for a while. There seemed to be no change in it whatsoever. The guests as well as the Petersons all remained where they were for the next few minutes, they then started to disperse and leave for their cars to go home. The party ended on a very abrupt note. In the end the Petersons were on their own as a family again. No one stayed.

'George, everyone has gone,' Jane said, looking over her shoulder.

'I don't blame them, what is that thing?' He asked.

'I don't know honey, do you James?'

James just stared at it seemingly without

blinking, almost in a trance-like state. He turned his head slowly towards his frightened parents.

'Something Bad.'

Chapter 2

Dear Diary,

It has been just the most surreal night I have ever known. It was a nice evening to begin with. It was nice mingling with some people that I haven't seen since last year's BBQ. Everyone was telling stories and making jokes. It was an all-round good atmosphere. We talked, ate, then talked some more.

When the night began to set in, things began to change. Young James Peterson came running outside and was looking up at the sky. There was a tense air which struck everyone at the same time as everyone began to follow his pointing finger. There, out of nowhere it seemed, was a light racing towards us. It moved very stealth like and was moving rapidly. The ground started to vibrate and then the light stopped dead still. It was so bright, though it was impossible to look away from its shine. It seemed to have everyone in a trace. Everyone was just staring at it. I looked behind and saw that people were leaving hastily. I continued to look up at the sky.

My head has begun to hurt once more. Just looking at the piercing light in the sky was enough to send pain to my head, like someone had hit me with something. I had no idea how long I was watching it for, minutes, hours, I have no idea.

With my head still pounding I sat on the couch. I felt and still do feel so scared. As I was sitting there, on the couch, I felt a lone tear trickle down my face. There are so many things going through my mind at the moment. I do not know what to think. It just arrived without any prior warning. No one could have foreseen this. This morning the weather man said it was going to be clear tonight. Instead of being clear, everyone is scared because a light had made its way down to us. There was no warning about it on any of the news stations I watched this morning. It just *appeared. Now I am scared, I do not know what to do next.*

I think that it is going to be a long night for everyone tonight. May as well pull up a chair and think of something which can help with the situation, although I fear that this thing might be here to stay.

Until next time...

The night was long for everyone in town who witnessed the coming of the light from space. Many people quickly took to social media websites to share their thoughts and theories on the mysterious light. Most were theories about an alien encounter. There was no media attention to everyone's surprise. There was no media at all. When something like this happened in the movies there was media coverage instantly, in real life there was nothing.

I wonder why the news station has not arrived. Jane thought. *Maybe the reporters panicked and went to be with family. Not that I blame them really. I would do the same.*

They all knew what they would say though. They would tell everyone not to panic, to carry on their lives like normal. But it wasn't normal. There was a light as bright as the sun in the sky. Bigger than the sun also at this distance. It was hovering no more than a couple of miles in the sky, seemingly mocking people of earth.

As the world span, so did the light. Many did not sleep that night. Most were spending their night in fear, looking up at the new arrival. There was no logical explanation. It came literally from nowhere in the space of an hour. It was a distant dot the size of a star then crept up on the unsuspecting earth and is now just... there.

James Peterson managed to fall asleep quickly after the excitement of the evening's events. He did not know what it was and his knowledge could not define what it was. He searched his notes and books for a while after the Petersons entered the house from outside. Nothing. He could find nothing. He promised himself before he went to sleep that he would check again in the morning. He did not tell his parents that he had no idea. He just simply didn't say anything when they came in. He went upstairs on his own mission and failed.

Downstairs in the lounge George and Jane pulled their seats up to the patio doors and watched the bright light for a while longer. Jane remained there all night just staring at it. George drifted off in the chair next to her.

Probably all that cooking, good night honey. Let us hope that this thing is not something too bad,

Jane hoped. She lifted George's hand up and wrapped it around her and she just stared in a trance at it. In the comfort of her husband's arm.

The light was coming from over the hills in the distance. The deep blue sky was now beginning to pale, slowly. Little by little the light in the sky got weaker and weaker. The birds began to sing and Jane could hear them through the patio doors, singing the morning song. The birds are able to carry on, nothing special happening to them. The birdsong continued. Jane could see from the comfort of her seat that the wind was not strong at all. It hardly moved the surrounding trees, it was going to be another hot day. The day was establishing itself more and more every second, it was getting lighter and lighter. The sky was nearly the colour of a tropical sea, a clear blue colour. The mysterious light which appeared had now faded to hardly anything. This pleased Jane, she was worried about James. James was her only child and a mother worried... a lot.

The time was six in the morning and the sky was reaching its final stage of blue. Jane had moved from her position she had kept all night to make coffee for herself and George.
James is not going to school today, was her

first thought. *Would the school even be open,* she wondered. She opened her phone to the internet page for his school. "Closed due to unforeseen circumstances".

In other words everyone crapped themselves and are spending the day with their loved ones, Jane smiled at her wisdom.

The kettle, which was on a rolling boil now, clicked to confirm that it was indeed hot enough for coffee time. She poured the water into both cups and went to the fridge for milk. On her way back to the cups she could smell something, something burning. She went swiftly to the lounge and saw nothing suspicious and then went upstairs to James' room. Nothing unusual. She could smell it getting more prominent. She went downstairs and straight out the front door. The smell hit her almost immediately, nothing looked unusual though.

Probably a strange side effect from the light, she walked into the house again and George was up and sipping his coffee.

'Mornin',' he said solemnly.

'Alright, can you smell that... like burning?' She asked.

'Yeah, I got up 'cause I thought you fell asleep cooking toast.'

'It's strange, nothing looks out of the ordinary.'

'Probably a side effect from that thing we saw

last night, have you seen it this morning? It's not half as bright,'

'I know...George?' she asked. 'There is something very wrong and strange going on, I don't like it. I fear it's going to scar James for life. What happens if it starts to like... I don't know, manifest into something dangerous and life threatening. I'm scared George. Really...scared,' she said the last words with emphasis. She was scared and her friends were scared and her son was scared, she could tell.

'I know honey. I'm scared too. Let's see what happens, if something does happen then we can deal with it when it does. Until then -,' his eyes dropped to his feet. 'Look, we can't do anything about it, try not to worry. I know you will, but try. We can't move it. If it has got something planned, we can't stop it,' He continued. Jane cried almost immediately after he finished talking and embraced George. They hugged so tight. They both could not remember a time when there had been so much emotion in a hug. They were scared for all their lives.

From the floor above, Jane and George heard the rumblings of James waking up.

'Let's try, for his sake,' George said looking towards the ceiling. Jane nodded in agreement at this. She got up and noticed that the smell of burning was dying down slightly, or maybe she was just getting used to it. Maybe she was over reacting to last night's events. She walked into the lounge and moved their seat back to where it was. It was easy to move sofas back to where they had been, you could see the feet marks left by the sofa in the carpet. After she moved it back she stood at the patio doors and just looked up. She could see that it was still there but not as noticeable against the bright background. This put her mind at rest slightly, made it easier to pretend. She looked out at the hills in the distance and could feel that there was something different. Something changed, she could not put her finger on it. She stared through tired and heavy eyes, desperately trying to find what was different, then James came down the stairs.

He entered the kitchen. Jane came in behind him.

'Mornin' son,' George said, failing to sound enthusiastic.

'I'll pour you some juice,' Jane said and walked towards the fridge. 'Sleep well?' She asked.

'Not too bad. I didn't dream, but I woke up a few times. That light, so bright, it kept waking me up,' James replied.

'Not to worry hun, as you probably guessed the school is closed for the, well… next few days,' she said and showed him her phone to prove this. As if proof was needed.

'I might go and speak with my friends online if you don't mind, after last night, I could do with some normality,' James said.

'Absolutely, I think that is just what you need,' Jane agreed. James sat at the table for a moment longer, finished his juice then got up and walked away. You could hear the *thumps* as he moved upstairs.

George and Jane just sat in silence for the rest of the morning, nothing needed to be said. Occasionally Jane would return to her place at the patio doors, staring up into the sky, also trying to find out what was different. She opened the double door which lead onto the back patio area. A gust of cool wind hit her, the smell of freshly cut grass and burnt wood was on the wind. The sun beat down on her face. The birds were still singing their songs in their nests. At the back of their lawn she could see a rabbit hopping its way further into the distance, then it disappeared underground. They always had rabbit holes in their garden. Jane liked this, it reminded her about all the other critters we share our planet with. She loved wildlife and animals. She always remembered when she was small, having aspirations about becoming a vet when she grew up.

She kept the doors open and re-entered the house and laid on the sofa. She drifted off to the sound of the great outdoors. Sleep took her almost instantly, she was so exhausted. She hoped that when she woke up everything would be as it was. In fact, she wanted the past couple of days to be a nightmare and wake up in her nice bed and carry on with her life.

It was cold and dark. She was laying on the floor of a cell type room. There was no sound, apart from that of a dripping pipe. It echoed through her mind. It was eerie.

There was a voice, it crept up on her. The words it spoke were fuzzy and hard to hear. There was no one there, but this voice was persistent. It kept coming into her brain, it seemed to be warning her about something, but then again maybe not. The voice sounded like one of fear, maybe it was her own voice. The sound of the dripping pipe persisted and it seemed to grow louder with every drop, the noise got into her mind and she found it hard to distract herself from it.

She sat up and looked around but could not see her hand in front of her face, the voices tapered. She then heard the sound of a handle turning and then a blinding, white light engulfed her and she found she was suddenly struck blind, unable to see anything. Yet she could still sense that there were some people approaching her, she could not see who it was, as her eyes were still blurry from the bright light. The people grabbed her and started to move her towards the white light, she managed to break free from their grasp.

She was again in darkness with the sound of the dripping pipe to keep her company.

Chapter 3

The air seemed cold, colder than any other night there had been. Jane opened her eyes slowly and scanned the room carefully. It took a few seconds for her eyes to adjust to the dark and remember she was in the lounge. She had fallen into a deep sleep and now it was dark outside. Looking at her phone to show the time, she winced back as the bright light struck her eyes, one-twenty in the morning. Jane looked towards the patio doors, where she could see something outside. She stood and walked towards them gingerly and drew back the thick curtain, she saw that the object in the sky was still there, although it was not shining as bright tonight, it did not make it any easier to accept it.

Jane unlocked the door and walked onto the patio area, the cool air wrapped around her as she did so. She just stood still taking in the sight of the thing, she then noticed that the wildlife was not making any sound at all. The smell of burning which had been noticed before still lingered in the air and she was still unsure of its origins. The object in the sky still hadn't moved its position, it was just there.

Jane remained where she was, just looking around for a while. Then she came into the house and locked the patio doors behind herself. She walked to the kitchen to pour some juice but found that it had all gone, the juice container was warm, left in the sun all day. Water from the tap it had to be. She opened the white cupboard and pulled out a clear crystal glass from the top shelf, then turned on the tap and filled the glass about half way. Taking a little sip, it was pure and cool in her throat as it travelled through her body, she could feel its path. She finished the rest off, then placed the glass in the sink. The house was silent, not one sound. It was unnerving just how quiet it was.

Jane made her way upstairs and as she passed James' bedroom she peeked in on him. She could see him in his bed, the duvet slowly rising and falling and the sound of his breathing filled the air. A hint of a smile appeared on her lips, she loved James so much and she would try not let the past couple of days impact his life. She had told herself this ever since the bright light came into their lives. She walked into the room, noticing that there were magazines everywhere. Sitting on the end of the bed her eyes watched her only son sleep. She looked around the room again, all his books were neatly packed on shelves. She bent down to pick up a magazine from the floor and had a little flick through, it was a magazine on space. Jane scanned some of the pictures to see if she could see the visitor, but could not. She placed the magazine back on the floor and kissed James on the head and returned to the hallway.

Opening the door to her own bedroom, she peeked in. The bed had a vacant space all ready for her, though she was not tired she got in all the same and pulled George close to her. Whilst hugging him, her eyes gazed over to the bedroom window, from this side of the house the object could not be seen and outside looked normal. But then what was normal? She could see a faint light illuminating off of the object from the back of the house but that was OK. Jane just watched and waited for the sun to arise again.

Jane looked at her phone again, seemingly moments later, it was six-thirty, she must have fallen back into a dreamless sleep. Now she was awake, she seemed to be more tired than before. George was still in his fetal position, asleep and snoring softly. He is so calm and collected, Jane wished that she could be the same but she was a worrier, she worried about almost everything. There would even be times she would worry about herself, although she would put on a front for James. She had done so all his life and tried to be as strong and confident as she possibly could, but he seemed to notice. Jane rolled onto her back and looked up at the ceiling. She stayed there for a while, then she heard something, someone walking around downstairs. It sounded like a chair moved along the kitchen floor.

James, he's up early, she thought. Jane got out of bed and walked towards the door, then turned to take in the sight of her loving husband once again. She could not live without him, he was her rock. Anything she wanted, she had. Jane turned the door knob and ventured into the hallway, then walked slowly towards the stairs and caught a glimpse of something in James' room. He was still in bed. She could still hear something coming from downstairs. Her heart sank in her chest, when she saw James still curled up in bed. Cautiously she walked to the top of the staircase and looked around, then took one step down but couldn't see anything. She continued to descend the stairs one at a time, all while looking and expecting to see someone, or something. Jane reached the foot of the stairs and turned to look into the lounge area, there she saw that the patio door was swinging open hitting against the frame in the wind. There seemed to be something sinister in the way that it moved, slowly swinging, then the bang seemed out of sync.

I'm sure I closed this, of course I did. She thought, standing in front of the doors. Doubt crossed her mind. She had went outside, she remembered that and was sure that she locked the door behind her upon re-entering the house, but just could not remember. She pulled the patio doors shut with a dull thump, it stayed shut. She could not help herself, Jane had to look up. There was something almost hypnotising about it, she could not understand. Although scared beyond belief, she was also interested in it.

A hand touch her shoulder which made her jump.

'Don't worry, just me,' it was George. 'I heard you get up and thought we could have some time on our own before James gets up,' he continued. She nodded in agreement and went to the kitchen to put the kettle on. Jane checked her phone's internet to see if James' school was still shut, the mobile was not picking up a good signal anymore. It struggled to bring up the homepage for the school, when it did the phone signal was lost, the internet crashed. She looked up at George and he shrugged his shoulders.

'I wonder how long the school is going to be shut,' she pondered.

'I don't know hun, probably until the teachers'

return, which could be tomorrow. Might never happen,' he said.

'I do hope it's soon, I've been thinking about what you said and I think that we need to carry on as normal, James needs to go to school and spend time with friends. We live so far away from anything here, it's starting to drive me insane, especially in light of the circumstances,' she said. George did not reply, instead he took a sip of coffee which Jane had put in front of him.

They remained quiet for a while, with no jobs to go to, their conversation was running a little dry, just like they were running low on supplies in the house, bread, milk, juice etc.

'I might take a little drive today and see if anyone is out and about,' George said. He was secretly worried about what he was going to do for work and wanted to check on his livestock outside the town also, but not before he found someone who might have a clue about what was happening.

'That's a good idea, I think I might join you. We will ask James as well,' Jane said, sounding almost excited. Jane felt awake at the idea, it was hard to feel excited, but she hadn't left the house in three days and was feeling a bit of cabin fever.

They sipped their coffee, savoring every last drop, the cups soon ran dry and George topped them up. It was the first time since the light came down, where they have actually felt normal. Just sitting at the table drinking coffee, the sun was shining once again outside, the world seemed like it was silent. There was no sign of any wildlife at all. The peace was nice though.

Jane finished her second cup and put the empty in the sink, next to her glass from last night. She turned and kissed George on the cheek. A humming sound could be heard from outside. They opened the door and saw that their backup generator had been started.

'Well, guess we are down to our last power supply,' Jane said.

'I guess so, I haven't topped it up for ages. I hope it will last for the duration.' Jane looked at him for a while, her heart sinking in her chest at the prospect of not having any power. It seemed, that at any moment they would be transported back in time, to a time without the luxury of electricity. They were fearful.

Dear Diary

The time is eight in the morning. It is the second day under the light. I have woken up feeling very peculiar. I feel like I haven't slept at all, my body aches, as if I had just ran a full marathon. I feel now that the light in the sky has made me exhausted. I had another strange dream last night.

I was in the Petersons house. The time was about six in the morning. I was wondering around, not knowing what for, just searching for something unknown. I was in the kitchen and took a seat on one of the wooden kitchen chairs. I sat there and stared out of the window, up at the paling blue sky. I felt like I could have stayed there forever, it was so peaceful. I continued to sit there, the clock above the kitchen door said it was six twenty five. I stayed a while longer.

Five more minutes must have passed, I was still looking out of the window, in a daydream. I heard some movement above me. A voice intruded my head.

'Get out, now,' it said to me. It sounded familiar, the voice. Was it my own? I was not sure. Without thinking I got up and began to run for the back doors. I hit my hip on another chair in the kitchen, which moved the chair along the floor creating a loud echoing sound. I ran as fast as I could out of the house.

Then I was blinded, blinded by the light. It went all fuzzy for a moment. I did not know what was happening.

I woke up in my chair, the one where I now sit. I had a pain in my waist, I looked and saw that my hip was coming out in a bruise. It was red and turning a blue colour. I must have been sleepwalking and bashed it on something. The dream felt so real.

I'm going to have a nap to try and sleep off this tiredness I feel. I can feel my eyes slowly drifting away. I will write again when I wake up, hopefully feeling refreshed.

Until Later...

Chapter 4

Feeling a sense of dread, fear and nervousness, George walked up to the patio doors which lead out back. He didn't exit the house but stood in the doorway and gazed up at the shape in the sky. It wasn't round, it had strange shaped edges.

Perhaps it is a satellite that has lost its course and came down to Earth. George thought. He knew this wasn't what it was. Someone would have come to see it or sort it out. George thought about that eventful night, how everyone had been so happy, they have not heard from any of their friends since. Memories of just standing there, turning and seeing this bright white light come towards them from the sky came flooding back. Everyone was sure it was going to make impact, but instead it just halted in the sky.

Walking out of the house, he noticed the smell of burning his wife first mentioned had now grown a little stronger. Someone burning rubbish, would be anyone's guess. But with the shape lingering in the sky, it was hard to think rational thoughts. When George turned his back to walk in, he could feel it, watching him. The shape in the sky, taunting him, mocking him. He felt like shouting up at it, but refrained himself, it would make Jane and James upset and nervous. He fought the urge to look back at it and carried on. He locked the doors behind him, rattling the handle to be sure it was locked.

He walked upstairs to where his wife was. She wasn't in the bedroom. He could hear the bath taps running. Good. This gave him time to think about things, think about where to travel today and see how much of an impact it has had on their little town.

Walking towards James' door, George pushed it open a little. He stared in at the dark shape moving around. James, stirring from sleep. He walked in and peeked through the gap in the curtains. He still saw the shape in the sky and quickly closed the gap again. James had fallen back to sleep again. George crept out of the boy's room and pulled the door closed.

Back in his room George felt an urge to just breakdown, cry, scream and shout. What would that achieve? He fought back the tears threatening in his eyes. He tried to think about happier times. He needed to stay strong for his family.

With difficulty he thought back to when he, himself was a boy. His dad would take him on long walks, up and down hills they trod. He and his dad did not talk much on these outings, there was just the sound of the wind blowing to accompany them. They would be out for hours, mostly on weekends. They would always walk the same path which took them to what felt like to a young George, the top of the world. They would ascend the steep hills and when they reached the top, the view was indescribable. It took his breath away every time. They could see their town sitting below, miniature model size. They would stay there for a little, then make their way back home for dinner.

George had a smile on his face thinking about those times. The urge to cry disappeared. He promised himself, that one day he would take his family to that hill. He pulled on some clean jeans and a clean shirt. No jumper required, the temperature was at its highest all year and rising still. He could still hear Jane in the bath so decided to make another coffee. The kettle was boiling, the water inside became energetic with the heat, after pouring the water in, he sipped.

Outside the wind was minimal and the trees did not move. The sky was a beautiful shade of blue, with not a cloud in the sky. The sun was around the other side of the house so there was nothing to obstruct his view, he felt he could stare out of this window forever. He sipped, then stared. Sipped again, then stared. George walked to the kitchen table and sat on it facing the window. He went into a daydream, it was a lovely feeling. He felt safe, nothing would harm him in this dream. All of a sudden he heard the loud sound of the lock from the bathroom and it snapped him out of it. George was back in reality.

With the sink filling with cups, he turned on the hot tap, letting out a stream of water. He added some washing up liquid and proceeded to clean what was in there. George put the cups and teaspoons in their designated space and walked once again to the patio. At first he had a happy feeling inside, until the shape reappeared in his line of vision. Happy turned to dread and nervousness once again.

'How long are you here for?' he whispered to it. Of course, there was no reply, but it made him feel better. He could hear the creaking of the floorboards above his head, Jane getting dressed. He felt trapped all of a sudden, walking from one room to another all day. With nothing else to do, his farming had stopped so he could be with his family. To help support them through this time. Jane's work had been suspended because all the doctors and nurses were spending time with their families and James' school was still shut. How many jobs and services had ceased due to this? He intended to find out.

George could hear Jane descending the stairs. He walked to the bottom to meet her.

'Ready?' he asked. She just nodded. He could see that, like him, she was scared, nervous and dreading what they may find.

'James is still asleep, we should leave a note,' she explained. She jotted down some words on a pad and then Jane turned to George signaling that she wanted to go. He opened the front door and they both walked out onto the front 'Welcome' mat. They just stood still for a minute. The air seemed thicker than it had been this morning, the heat was still rising and wouldn't peak until lunchtime. They walked towards their car. George clicked the button on his key to open it and they slipped inside. He turned the key in the ignition, the car started and the radio blasted a loud sound for a second, then the whole thing cut out and the sound was reduced to static. They both glanced at each other. George quickly turned off the system and they both resided in silence.

'What is happening?' Jane asked.

'I have no idea,' he replied.

They both just sat there staring at the object looming over their house. It was unnerving, like something out of a science fiction movie. He then maneuvered the car around and then drove away from the house. George and Jane both felt their breath escape them.

Chapter 5

James awakened at the sound of the front door closing. He sat up in his bed and looked around at his room, sighed and swung his feet around to touch the floor. He stood up and stretched. The room smelled like sweat and like something had perished. Making his way to the curtains he threw them open to let in the daylight, the sun hit him and had to look away from the powerful light. With the area bathed in light, illuminated dust particles could be seen. They floated carelessly around in the room so he cracked open the window slightly. The smell of the air was one of burning, the breeze which had hit his face was warm. James stared out of the window for a little longer, then looked up at the bright sky and saw the object floating there. He was not too worried or scared about it, although curious, he felt they would deal with something when it happened.

James made his way to the bathroom, then downstairs and spotted a note on the kitchen table. The house was so quiet and it made him feel slightly uneasy. It had been a few days being in the house with his mother and father, now they were nowhere to be seen, it felt unusual. He walked towards the note and unfolded the paper which said simply 'James'.

'Myself and dad just popped out to see what's happening in town. Shouldn't be too long. Do NOT go outside, Love you. Mum.'

James was not initially thinking of going outside but the thought that it was like forbidden fruit made it desirable. He pushed the thought away and grabbed some water from the tap. Grabbing a warm glass from the drying rack, he filled it. The water was cold and the glass was warm, it caused the glass to produce instant condensation, fascinated by this, he watched. He watched for a while, hypnotised by the glass of liquid in front of him. He was interested in science, loved studying elements, chemicals and more excitingly the reactions elements and chemicals made.

James sipped at his breakfast drink and went into the lounge, sat on the sofa and turned on the TV... nothing, He changed the channel... nothing. There was no signals found on any channels, what was produced was the constant picture of white and grey pixels which danced around the screen. The radio stations were also just static. He turned the television off.

He stood up and with nothing else to do, approached the patio doors. Looking up at the sky, he just stared at it, it almost seemed like it was beckoning him to come outside. James caught a glimpse of a lone rabbit running into a hole in the ground, there were no birds in sight, all was quiet. He looked far down at the end of the garden to where the hills were, James liked looking at the hills, they were peaceful and seemingly untouched. Perfect. Today, however, there seemed to be something off with the landscape, his brain was desperately trying to figure out what it could be. It annoyed him when no conclusion was made. He had looked at the hills every day since he was a baby, still when something had changed, his eyes defied him.

Why had the news reporters not been here, taking pictures or whatever? Why has the prime minister not made any statements? Surely they must have protocols in place for this sort of thing. He thought about it. All the movies he had watched and all the TV shows he had watched, when something like this happens it gets media attention all the time. He unlocked the door and opened it, it smelled like burning even more now. Walking around the back of the house, there was no other signs of life. No one else was here.

It was quiet outside, not even the company of the birds singing their morning song. There was a slight breeze but it wasn't enough to make the trees move or make any sound. James felt scared just then and went back into the lounge. Locking the door behind him, he gazed at the outside world from the safety of his home.

Maybe it is some kind of bio-weapon from the government trying to test the people, he went on to think. But it sounded ridiculous so he soon pushed it to the back of his mind.

He ascended the stairs again and sat at his computer, pressing the power switch, nothing happened. He tried again, the same outcome. There was no power to the computer at all, the standby lights were off. James rushed downstairs and out to the generator, just in time to hear the motor fade and then stop. Without the sound of the hum, the silence was even more unnerving.

James entered the house again and it began to get dark for a moment as a cloud passed over, the light of the sun ceased. It transformed the whole house, it was difficult to see. He flicked a nearby light switch but nothing happened. Many bad thoughts crossed his mind in a matter of seconds. He was literally on his own now, he knew it. There was no communication with the outside world at all, the phones were dead, the internet not working, nothing. Moments later the sun appeared again from behind the cloud and the house was bright again, but he knew that when the sun set, there was no electric to light the house with, it was going to be cold and dark.

Chapter 6

On their way to town Jane and George saw no one. They took the two mile journey slowly, as slow as they could, so that they could watch and see if anyone was out and about, they saw no one. The closer they got to the middle of the town the less countryside was seen and what replaced the view were small townhouses. The grey stone on the front of them made the atmosphere more depressing. Some of the houses had planters outside the windows, which brightened it up a little. They both watched with a detailed eye to find any sign of life, but they could not find anything. Jane thought that she saw a curtain move as they went past a little detached cottage. She had to look twice, but there were no further movement that she could see.

They carried on their journey. The road which they were travelling on took them towards the petrol station, the big red sign shone out like a beacon, leading the way. The station would be their first stop. The road was bumpy. George signaled the car to go into the garage, but there was no need, no one else was on the road, habits. They saw a light on inside, parked the car and both got out simultaneously.

'I wonder if they are still open for business,' George said to himself, who looked at Jane. She just stared back and shrugged her shoulders at him. They both walked towards the building, it had big windows to see inside and it had automatic doors on the front. As they walked towards the doors the air suddenly got very cold, a wind blew and the smell of burning made its way up their noses. They both sniffed and looked at each other. The doors were not working when they approached them. They peeked into the station and saw no one around. There was a variety of items all over the floor. People must have been in a rush when the object appeared, there were tires and all sizes of nuts and bolts scattered around the floor. Both Jane and George walked the perimeter of the shop and found nothing or no one. They had another look inside.

'Hello... anybody there?' George called, no reply. He banged on the front doors but no one came.

A buzz sounded from the store, it was silent again for a while, then the lights in the station blew, creating a bang and pop sound. Jane jumped at the sudden noise. The whole petrol station was now in complete darkness, they could not see the back of the shop, even in the light of day.

'I'll go round the back and see if I can get in that way. If we can get these pumps working, we can fill our generator,' George said.

'I'll come with you, I feel a bit creeped out by all this,' Jane said. The two of them went around to the back and saw that the service door was slightly ajar, George forced it open to enter. Upon entering they found it difficult to see anything. They stumbled over boxes and wooden pallets and eventually reached the front section of the shop. Jane saw where the controls were behind the counter, she walked towards them and flicked the switch, nothing. She pressed some of the buttons, but these had no effect.

Something could be heard, coming from the far corner of the station. George followed the sound gingerly.

'Hello?' He called, having no reply. He could still hear the sound, like crisp packets rustling. Reaching the source of the sound, his heart pounded when two big black eyes looked up at him. All that could be seen was a silhouette of a big German Shepherd. Panicking, he backed up.

'Jane, get out,' he called. Jane took his advice and screamed his name as she charged through the shop, pushing aside the creates left out. George continued backing away slowly, he stumbled over a tyre left in the middle of the floor. Reaching out he caught hold of a display unit which tumbled to the floor with him. The crashing sound startled the dog and made it bark uncontrollably. Before George could get to his feet, he felt a shocking pain in his leg. Looking down he could see the dog clamped onto his muscle. He kicked out to free himself from the beast.

Outside Jane could only watch in horror as the animal was attacking. With one final forceful kick he was released and pushed the debris from his body as fast as he could. Getting up he ran to the back door, feeling pain in his leg with the pressure. Reaching the outside he slammed the door shut and as he staggered around to the front of the station, he could hear the dog scratching at the metal door, eager to get out.

Jane and George turned around back towards the car and slowly walked to the vehicle feeling deflated. Jane looked back one last time, it was just a dark shell which stood there. They sat in the car and just stared again at the station. George rolled up his trouser leg and saw puncture marks, slowly oozing with blood. He wiped it clean with a handkerchief, wincing at the pain.

'I hope that dog never had anything,' he said.

The sky overhead became dark as the sun was

hidden behind some passing clouds. The object could be seen, but looked more like a shadow in the dark sky.

'We must be mental hanging around this town on our own. Everybody probably went to be with their families,' Jane said.

'On to the next stop then I suppose, there has got to be someone here.' Jane did not say anything, she told herself not to get her hopes up. What if there is no one else in the town? This was a question which crossed both of their minds. Neither of them said it, neither of them needed to.

Chapter 7

Just down the lane a little was Property Road, home to the town's fish and chip shop "Codey's", also the convenience shop and the car parts shop, "Pipes". They pulled up in a little layby just alongside, all businesses were in darkness. All of the buildings had big commercial windows which allowed people to look inside. They both got out in unison, George grabbed a torch he had in the boot of the car and walked towards the first of the shops which was the convenience store. They approached it and Jane tried the door.

Surprised that it was opened, Jane and George entered and scanned the area. The shop had baskets all over the floor, some items pushed off shelves and bottles smashed, glass was everywhere. Both were surprised at how empty it was. The fridges did not have even a single drink in them. There were empty food shelves, all that remained was some crushed crisps which had been opened. The smell of beer and wine filled the air, it was stale. The floor was sticky with drying alcohol.

'Hello?' Jane called, with no reply.

'We are not having much luck here hun,' George said.

'Nope.' Just then they heard a noise come from the back of the shop, they followed the sound cautiously. Under the light of the torch, Jane noticed there were rat dropping all over the floor and had seen one running along where the food had fallen off the shelf. The noise they heard, which was like sniffing, was getting louder as they got closer. Afraid that there was another animal waiting for them, they both braced themselves for whatever it could be.

They looked around into what was probably an office of some kind, but did not see anyone. Still the sniffing sound continued. They carried on walking.

'Hello,' she said again. Nothing except this noise. She saw something move. Then saw what the noise was, it was rats scraping the walls. They were everywhere, someone who was in a rush to get out when the object fell, had left some biscuits and fruit out of a lunchbox and it was covered in ravenous rats, the smell was foul and sickly. It felt like their eyes were burning from the smell. Jane just left the shop as soon as she possibly could, George trailing behind, he tripped, igniting the shooting pains in his leg left from the bites. He shone the light on what was a box of fireworks. He got up and wobbled out of the shop to follow Jane. On the verge of tears, she stormed back to the car and told George to check the other two buildings.

He went to the next outlet which was "Codey's" but could instantly see that there was no one in it. The lights again had blown and both the service door and the front door was locked. He still knocked but no one answered for him, then moved along to the final outlet in the street, which was "Pipes" the car specialist.

This shop, just like the convenience store was open, he walked in. He felt uneasy on his own. The smell of car air fresheners filled the front of the shop, whereas towards the back it had a greasy sort of smell. There were no rats to be seen, of course, there was no food here. George shone the torch to every corner to see if there were signs of anybody, but he did not find anything interesting.

'Hello, if anyone is there please let me know.' No one replied. The shop was silent. He walked out and went back to the car where Jane was getting herself under control.

'No luck, no one around,' he said.

'Well, there are two other places that we could look. I think there will be people in those places. What do people do when something bad happens?' she asked. He shrugged. 'Drink or pray, I bet we find people at the pub or the church,' she continued. He liked the way she was thinking. They journeyed the mile or so to get to their next destination, their last destination. On the way they searched and still could not see anyone. Not even the animals were playing on the street, no children loitered on street corners, nothing. The smell of burning filled the car through the air conditioner. The clouds above cleared and the sky was blue again. Jane caught a glimpse of the sun and by the sun, still staring down was the light. It made her want to cry, but she held back the tears in her eyes.

They both watched the steeple of the church grow larger and larger the nearer they got. Before they knew it they were sat in between the church and the pub. George pulled up his trouser leg again to check the wound, it was beginning to scab over. He reached into the glove compartment to get out a tissue, dabbed it on his tongue and dabbed the wound to clean it.

'Ready?' Jane asked.

'Yeah, as good as I ever will be.'

'Right, just to speed things up, I'll take the church, you take the pub,' she said. He agreed. They both got out of the car and split up in opposite directions.

Chapter 8

Dear Diary,

I feel like I am losing my mind. I have no idea what is happening. I'm finding it hard to keep up with what is real and what is not. After my last entry in here, I fell asleep quite quickly. I do not know how long I slept for, maybe a couple of hours.

I woke up and I was wet with sweat. The room was dead silent. It took a minute for my eyes to adjust and then I realised I was in a different house from my own. I looked around and did not notice who's it was. There was a musty smell in the air. The curtains let in some light which highlighted the many dust particles floating around. I was glad when I saw that this notepad was still in my breast pocket of my jumper, I feel like I need to write everything down, so I could prove what is happening. To prove to myself that I am not going around the bend.

The house where I sat was silent. There was no humming from any electrical equipment, even though the plugs said that they were on. I realised soon after that all the electric had blown. I looked around the house, mainly to see who it belonged to. There were a few pictures hung up around the place, but no one that I recognised in them.

I was looking around a few minutes before I heard something from outside, a car. I hastily went to the living room window and pulled back the curtain a little so I could see out. It was the Petersons driving down the road. I looked for a moment longer, then Mrs. Peterson looked in my direction. I backed away from the window as fast as I could, so she did not see me. I hope she didn't. I don't want her thinking that I broke into someone else's house.

I am aware that this is completely insane, me just waking up in someone else's house. I do not know what is happening to me. It *seems that ever since that light came down to rest above our quiet little town I do not know what I am doing half the time. I feel like I have no control over my life anymore. I have lost so much weight but every time I try and eat I vomit. Also, as I have mentioned before, my sleep has been extremely altered. What is real? I have no idea anymore. Even now I can feel myself drifting off, I hope the people who lived here don't mind me sleeping on their sofa for a while. I just want to wake up and for the last two days to be one big outlandish nightmare, though somehow I do not think that is going to happen.*

I will write again later, when I get my head around this...

Jane approached the gate of the church yard. She stood in the entrance, scanning her surroundings. The perimeter of the church was marked with black iron wrought fencing and had gothic style black iron wrought gates. She moved into the churchyard with anticipation, immediately feeling the dark atmosphere of the graveyard, washing over her as she stepped in through the gates. She continued to look around to find any sign of life, nothing. Only the silence and the many grave stones were keeping her company.

There were many grave stones which marked those who have long been deceased. Most of the stones were damaged beyond recognition, the writing commemorating the body now distorted, over time and many seasons. An old oak tree stood in the sea of grave stones, it looked unnerving. A picture from a fantasy book. The oak tree had quite a large trunk which had grown distorted and twisted over the long decades which it has survived. It put Jane on edge just looking at it. Delving closer to the church she noticed that there was no sound, just the wind whistling around the graves. No birds were in the sky at all. None were even hiding in the trees.

The church was dark and the exterior had the classic grey bricks. It had a tall steeple which seemed to reach the heavens itself. Right on the top there was a rusty metal cross which marked God's house. There were many stained glass windows at the front face of the old building, some of the windows were cracked and many looked old and tired. As she approached the gothic doorway to the church, Jane felt a chill run down her spine. She looked around, feeling like there was someone watching her, though no one was around. She could see George just approaching the front door to the old looking tavern and turned back to the doors of the church. One was standing slightly ajar and she pushed it open.

The door creaked on its hinges as it swung open, the noise echoed through the old building, then the silence overtook the sound and it was quiet once more. The cold air inside rushed out and hit Jane. She felt scared and nervous about entering, even finding herself turning away to go, she thought and then turned to continue into the church. Jane was dreading what she might find inside or may not find, as the case may be. She had a bad feeling, she could not shake it and it would not leave. Jane entered.

Beyond the front door there was another door which lead to the main room of the church. Opening the door just a crack so she could look in, there was a ghostly breeze which ran along her face. She could not see anyone inside. The air was even colder in the main room.

Maybe everyone actually has gone, she thought and opened the door fully, whilst searching for anyone or anything to indicate a presence.

'Hello?' she called out, no one answered. She moved into the main room and noticed that the pews were untouched and in perfect position. On some, towards the back, dust lay carelessly on the polished wood. There was nothing unusual about it, apart from the fact that it was empty. There was old style candle chandeliers hanging from the roof of the building and there were candles on the walls. She walked down the aisle, towards the alter. The wind blew in through the thin cracks in the walls and windows, howling when the gusts got going. A door closed within the church somewhere. It echoed through the old building, even shaking the ground beneath her feet. She felt her heart pounding in her chest at the unexpected sound. It was so out of the blue she could not tell where it was coming from.

'Can I help you?' a voice asked. Jane jumped at the voice, then turned and saw Father Michael standing towards the back of the main room, by the front door.

'Oh thank heavens, there are others around,' she said. She was happy to see someone else in town, so happy in fact, tears threatened at her eyes. Jane barely managed to keep herself together.

'Oh yes, I have no family to be with at this horrible time, I will stay here for now. I believe God will protect me and I will protect him when the time comes,' Father Michael was a middle aged man. His hair was starting to go grey but he never had many wrinkles apart from small ones around his eyes. He looked good, but the recent event in town had started to take its toll on his appearance. He wore his dog collar and a black robe which travelled down to his shoes.

'I'm so glad I have found someone, is there anyone else in town?' she asked.

'Not that I know of. I haven't seen a soul. I think that they have all gone. Of course I do not know that for definite, but my gut tells me everyone is gone.'

'Gone? Gone where?'

'Out of town, to be with family and friends probably. They are all most likely sat at God's table now.' he said. Jane never replied but her face asked her question for her. 'The world outside this town has been destroyed,' he continued.

'What do you mean destroyed? I don't understand,' she sat down in shock and confusion.

'You don't know then,' he said. She was sitting forward and listened to every last word. The whole of the church was silent, it seemed even the walls were listening.

Chapter 9

Father Michael sat beside Jane on the front pews. He held her hand, just for a moment. His hands warm, hers icy cold. They sat in silence for a while, listening to the sounds of the old creaky church. The wind was creeping in through cracks in the windows, which were made over time and the wind whistling through the seams of the doors. The atmosphere got darker, coldness was setting into their bones. The sky outside slowly seemed to become gloomier. Though the temperature was still rising as the day continued, but she still felt colder than ever.

'What happened here... in this town? Why do you think that everyone who left are now...*gone*?' she asked, breaking the silence like the sound of shattered glass breaking on tiled flooring. Her voice echoed through the building, it made Jane herself jump.

'I'm not saying everyone is gone, but judging from what is happening outside the town I'm just being realistic. Sure some are maybe taking shelter underground, but without supplies they would not last very long. They might survive if... if that thing goes away,' he replied, looking out of a nearby window at the light sitting in the sky. Jane sat motionless and quiet, she did not say anything. She thought about going to get George so that he could listen, but her body was frozen with fear and couldn't seem to move, so she just listened.

'I can see by the look on your face that you are totally confused Mrs. Peterson,' he continued. She remained to sit in silence.

'I'll start from the beginning.'

'The evening that... thing arrived, I was in here having a meeting with some townspeople about improving the exterior of the church. I remember the sun shone through the stained glass windows, it felt heavy on my body. The sky was a bright pink colour, it made the whole church turn rosy. The birds could be heard from the old oak tree outside and children could be heard playing in the courtyard.'

'The conversations began to get boring and the room began to feel fuzzy, I felt so tired. I just wanted to be at home. Still I tried to keep in on the conversation as best I could. My eyes kept moving towards the window. It was so beautiful.'

'The conversation still flowed an hour or so later and the sky was becoming a dark colour. The sun was just disappearing outside and the night began. Some time went by and I was becoming restless, more restless than before. The sky was completely dark now, but a bright light still shone high up in the sky. I excused myself from the meeting and went to the bathroom, mainly for a break. Whilst in the bathroom, I opened up the window, the night outside was silent, I heard owls in the trees. There were few stars out, but still the atmosphere was bright. I washed up and took my seat back at the table. The meeting was closing and my head hurt, it was pounding, I could feel my heartbeat going through my head and just wanted to lock up and lay down.'

'Everyone exited the church to go home, although I turned off the lamps, the church was still bright. I walked to the main door and opened it a crack and there it was, a bright light in the sky. In that moment I remember feeling so many emotions at the sight; fear, nervousness, depression, clarity. I looked to God for an answer to what this was... that bright light.'

'I prayed as I stared at it, just hanging there in the sky. It got closer and then stopped and remained in this place, even now. I stayed in the church that night, thinking people may want to visit for answers but no one did that first night. I was surprised, I was sure many people look to God during their lives, religious or not. It turns out that people are not as open minded as they used to be, they did what many people did that night, went to be with family or friends. But I stayed, my faith was and still is being tested and bent to breaking point, I was going out of my mind trying to figure out what it was... no answer came to me. Sleep finally took over my body and it sent me to a dreamland, where no one or nothing could hurt me.'

'The next day I woke to sounds of cars beeping their horns outside, I walked to the front door and opened it. I noticed the object in the sky was still there. People were driving out of town, not many mind, most people probably left the night before. I could smell burning in the air and walked outside. I closed the doors and wandered down the path to the gates, walking down the path towards the town line, it was quiet and unnerving. A couple of cars passed me, but very far and few between.'

'The town line from here is about half a mile or so. I walked the distance and I had a sense of dread come over me when I reached the edge of town and was just speechless. The world outside the town was charred and singed, it looked as though the world was a big bonfire. The trees were still smoldering and the ground was dusty and covered in ash. I was surprised at how little smoke was rising from it all, I did not have any indication what was happening until I got close. I walked past the town line and the atmosphere became instantly very hot, still I continued walking. From what I could see the next town over had been destroyed, burned to cinders. The houses were burnt out, there were no people around. I entered one house and called out for anyone, but no one replied to me. I continued through the house and I saw a hand laying on the floor. Approaching it, I saw that it was a corpse. Burned and lifeless. It looked so painful, I said a prayer for the soul and I walked back out the house. I tried to call someone to help, but the phone line was busy, as I thought it would be.'

'With haste I got back to the church, I called up some of my contacts around the country, they answered and they explained that their towns and cities were slowly crumbling, slowly burning down. Their landmarks were cracking with the extreme shift in the atmosphere. They got word from other countries and it was the same story. I spent the rest of the day sending emails, trying to get word out, telling them about our seemingly unaffected town, we seem to be the only town in the world not affected. I doubt that the emails were received though. Shortly after, the electric went dead in the church. I am also aware that the whole town now is without electric.'

'Yesterday I had a visit from a lovely couple. I had not seen them before. I cannot remember their names. They were considering leaving town to be with their family. I did all I could to convince them to stay. I have no idea what they decided to do. Last night I cried, thinking I was the only one here. I know that this is a lot to take in Mrs. Peterson, but I think that you need to know. I am aware you have a son, make sure he does not leave the town. Whilst we stay in Merryville, I believe that God will protect us. I'm not saying that we are completely safe here, but we are not burning yet.'

Chapter 10

As the doors closed at the church, George turned to face their local public house, 'The Hill's Angel'. With the look of the old style building from the outside, it looked like any other pub in the country, though to George it felt haunted. Haunted, not by ghosts but from how quiet it was. Even looking at the pub in the quiet air sent shivers running down his spine. The windows were old, tired and breaking at the seals. The roof was thatched and it sloped down on one side, nearly reaching the floor. The sign up above the front doors, swung on its supports, creating an unsettling screeching sound.

The temperature was hot, mid to high thirties. The wind was minimal, but when it blew it cut through the air like a knife through butter. There were flower planters at the front, though the flowers were slowly wilting, heat and lack of care were slowly killing them.

George did not feel very optimistic about this adventure, especially when he approached the front doors. He proceeded with automatic caution as he had felt on edge since... that night, when that light came to them. George started opening the front door, as he did so it squeaked making a high pitched noise on its hinges. All was deadly quiet inside, unsettling almost. Tables were left unattended, unclean. The smell of stale drinks hit him instantly. Looking around he could see broken glass on the floor and wine glasses which had been knocked over. Uneaten bar snacks left abandoned here and there, a single rat could just be seen in the corner of his eye, scurrying away to safety. The rat would surely continue his feast when George was again out of sight.

'Hello?' He called. As expected there was no answer. George ventured further and the smell of spoilt food and drink made him heave, swarms of flies circulated the air. The air felt thick because the smell was so bad. He felt like he could vomit at any moment and tried his hardest to hold the feeling back, try to think of something else, but the smell was so sweet and so bitter at the same time, it was almost impossible to not think about it. He held his sleeve to his face to cope with the smell and moved on.

Now in the middle of the bar, more rats and mice could be heard in the wall cavities and nibbling on crisps from different corners of the room. No one was in sight, he decided to look behind the bar for anything of interest but found nothing. Just more broken glasses and spilt drinks. Other than that and also the lack of people, nothing else seemed out of place. He decided that the idea of finding anyone here was a waste of time, but just in case he continued to investigate the rest of the building. Out the back, behind the bar area was a staircase, which George guessed led to the guest rooms. There was also a door slightly ajar, he could see the start of the stairs descending to the basement area.

He pushed the door fully open and tried the light. There was nothing as he had expected. Turning on his torch, he made it two steps down before the batteries died. He walked back into the bar area and searched high and low for a flash light or lighter or something. The shelves were sticky and the stench coming from them smelt like something had surely expired. After much searching he stumbled across a box of matches, laying by one of the tills. George walked back to the basement doors to resume his search.

Striking a match, he descended the first few steps and stopped. More rats could be heard running around, scavenging for food. Carrying on his decent, the air got colder the further underground he went. Reaching the bottom, another match was struck, it was clear that no one was here. A few stray rats ran around but that was it. He climbed back up the stairs to the ground level, glad to leave the rats behind. Deciding to leave the basement door open to try and clear the sickly smell a little, George gingerly walked up the flight of stairs to the guest rooms.

The pub only had two rooms for rent. He walked to the first door and to his surprise it opened first time. Stepping into the spacious, clean bedroom, the air was much fresher. It was so orderly and tidy, a complete contradiction to the downstairs bar area. Looking at the bed, tiredness crept up on him. Shaking the feeling he continued searching the room, but there was no one around.

He walked back out into the hallway and the smell instantly hit him all over again, George doubled over and vomited. He stayed where he was for a few minutes, waited for his stomach to settle, then carried on down the hallway carefully. The second door also opened first time, it looked identical to the previous room, clean and fresh. There was nothing of interest, it had the smell of deodorant in the air. George walked over to the room's big window, which looked out onto the church and wondered how Jane was getting on.

A sound.

George spun around and looked out into the

hallway, nothing was there. He walked with haste down the corridor to the top of the stairs, forgetting about the dull pain in his leg.

'Hello?' He called again... nothing. Noticing that there were no other rooms to look in he walked slowly down the stairs, the sound appeared again. He followed, it was coming from the main bar area. Walking with his eyes constantly darting around for any movement. He slowly and anxiously entered the main bar area... no one was around.

Feeling a little uneasy, George walked to the entrance and stepped into the sunny outdoors. The sun beat down on his face, the cool breeze seemed like heaven. He could still smell the burning odour in the air, but it sure beat the smell of the pub.

Walking back over to his car and sitting in the driver's seat, he looked up at the sky. He could still see it floating overhead, staring down at him, taunting him. He felt angry just looking at it.

What the hell is it? Why had it come? These were the questions that have been going around his mind since the arrival. Nearly two days have passed since it had come and still they had no answers. He stared towards the church and wondered if Jane was OK, sure she would be.

No one here anyway, he thought, then closed his eyes. The afternoon sun was hitting the car and the heat was relaxing, tiredness overtook his power to stay awake. A dreamless sleep caught him.

Chapter 11

'This is all wrong,' Jane said.

'I'm afraid it is the truth,' Father Michael assured her. The air, although hot, felt so cold to Jane, getting colder by the second. Each time she thought about what was happening, a little colder she felt. Too shocked by what he was telling her, she wanted to cry. A single tear managed to escape her eye and slowly trickled down her face and stopped where her mouth started.

'What are we supposed to do now?' She asked, trying to fight further tears that threaten her eyes.

'Pray, I have no other suggestion. Our faith will guide us.'

'I just... can't,' she said looking around the church. She felt so small and helpless. More tears threatened. She wiped what had gathered in her eyes.

'You must try,' he said calmly. 'We can pray together. Come with me to the alter.'

Father Michael stood up and walked to the alter

and prayed. Although his faith had been extremely tested over the last couple of days, he refused to give up. Silence...it felt so loud in the old building. He turned to Jane, but she was already pacing towards the front doors. Just as he stood up to call out to her, the front door slammed shut.

Out in the car George was still asleep. Jane got into the passenger door and thumped it shut, unaware that George was napping. This startled him and he jumped and was ready to go almost instantly. Noticing the moisture on her face, which glistened in the sunlight, he knew she had been crying. Her eyes were puffy and red.

'Are you OK?' he asked.

Jane just stared up at the sky, at the thing... just floating there. Taunting, plotting maybe. The sun was starting to descend in the sky.

'Drive to the edge of town,' she instructed. George could see she was upset and did what she wanted. He felt dread all over his body almost instantly. He did not ask, he had a feeling he would soon find out why. He turned the key in the ignition and revved the engine a little.

He pulled out onto the main road, whilst looking both ways. He smirked to himself after he did it. No one around, although some habits die hard. George glanced over at Jane, she was in a daze, not really looking at anything in particular, just staring into space. The more he thought about the situation, the more worried he became. He knew that their circumstances was bad, but he could never have braced himself for just how bad it was. The scale of it never crossed his mind.

As they approached the town line the smell of burning grew stronger, it was coming through the windows in the car, nearly choking them as it did. Not a word was exchanged between George and Jane. The silence said more than words could. Just before reaching the town line they both noticed the change in the trees. Changing from a luscious green colour to a brown, then finally to a char black. Still no words were passed, Jane burst into tears at the sight of what laid before her.

They both looked out at the devastation where the town ends and the next begins. The trees were burned to a cinder, the few lone houses that were in view seemed like burnt out shells. Everything had the feel of a real life scene from an apocalypse movie. In the road laid a few rats, foxes and birds which had been rapidly dehydrated and burned to death on the warm road surface. George hadn't noticed before, but this morning had not started with the sound of birdsong.

Surely they are not all dead? I wonder if my livestock are dead also? He thought. He knew the answer and tried not to think about it. Jane was still upset, hysterical actually. Laughing and crying at the same time. She looked up and then back towards the debris. Everywhere, complete carnage.

'This was all caused by... by that?' He pointed up at the shape in the sky. Jane did not respond with words, she just nodded the confirmation. George held Jane in his arms for a minute. He had many more questions to ask, but did not want to upset Jane even more then she already was.

He turned the car around as the sun began to make its final decline of the day, the sky was a honey colour with streaks of pale pink shooting through.

The journey homeward bound was silent. Jane had stopped crying and was looking out of the window. She wondered what could have done this to them, what could of caused this much devastation in such a little time. Also wondering why this town was the only one, not just in England, but in the world. The whole world had gone to hell.

They pulled into the driveway of the house. George turned off the engine and they sat in silence for another minute or so. George held Jane's hand while they both stared at their home. They had both worked so hard to keep this roof over their head, now it seemed that it was all a waste of time.

IT was shining bright tonight.

Dear Diary,

I feel that I am going crazy, quickly. I have just woke up in the comfort of my own house. The dark has closed in outside and the only thing I can see is the light from the sky.

My head is pumping with pain, I feel dizzy. I feel like I am not in control anymore. I have no idea what I am doing half the time.

After I fell asleep in that stranger's house I had another dream.

I was in 'The Hill's Angel' pub, just on the outskirts of town. It was quiet, deadly silent in fact.

I was there a while, then I heard the humming of an engine ticking along. I looked out of the big bay window and saw it was the Petersons again. I hastily went upstairs to where the guest bedrooms were, I found them locked. I wanted to get a better view from the bedroom window. I searched through the broken glass and spilt drinks under the till until I came to the section for bedroom keys. I grabbed both and returned upstairs.

I unlocked the first bedroom I came to and immediately saw that there was no facing window in there, I walked out straight away and shut the door behind me, before walking to the other guest room. I used the other key I obtained and entered briskly. I walked towards the window which looked out towards the parish church. I nosed at what the Petersons were doing. I saw Jane pottering around outside the church entrance. She turned to face the pub, almost looking at me. I wondered if she saw me. I was hidden by a brilliant white net curtain. I could not see George anywhere. She entered the church and at the same moment I heard a noise come from below me.

I heard George walking around downstairs. He called to say 'hello' but I could not answer. I do not know why, I just couldn't. There was something inside me stopping me from contact. There was a voice in my head warning me not to get caught. It was so strange...it did not sound like my voice.

I went to the guest room door and closed it far enough so I could just peek out still. I could hear a door open somewhere else in the pub. I still could not see him, I waited. Moments later I could hear footsteps on the stairs and he emerged.

He came across the first guest room and entered it. Luckily I did not lock it behind me. I crept out from my spot, knowing he was going to look in the room where I was next. I managed to get past the doorway and down the stairs without making a sound or being seen.

Reaching the downstairs I could hear him walking around upstairs. I stopped behind the bar just for a second or two. I was out of breath from all the adrenaline and wanted to take in some long breaths.

'Get out now,' the voice said to me.

I ran around the bar, in doing so tripped on an upturned barstool, this created a crash. George must have heard me, he called down after. I did not stay around long enough to hear what he said. I managed to get out of the front door undetected. A big flash of white light. I woke up in my chair at home again.

Even though I have just woke up I am starting to think that I am not dreaming these things at all. I think that all this is really happening. I just cannot figure out the reason why I do not want to be seen so badly. I want to be with people, especially if they may have answers to what is happening around here. I do want to be seen, but I won't let myself. I am going to go insane trying to figure it out. Something else that is weird is that I went to sleep in the other house and woke up in my own, I even have the diary entry to prove that it was real. I have no idea what happens in-between blacking out and waking up. I do not remember how I got home. I don't even remember leaving my house. I just turn up at these places, stay a while, then go somewhere else.

I can feel my body ache, I haven't eaten anything substantial in over two days. The headaches I have been having are making me feel sick and they are getting worse every day. I feel like I have no control. It feels like someone else is walking in my legs, thinking in my brain and speaking from my vocal cords.

I think I will try and stay awake for a while. I am so exhausted though, I do not know how long I will last. I feel like I haven't slept in days.

Maybe I Haven't

I will write again when I have found some more energy, even writing this is making me feel tired.

Until next time...

Chapter 12

It was the third day since the object in the sky arrived. The Petersons, unable to sleep, were just staring at each other round the kitchen table. They were all wondering how it got this bad, so quickly. Their whole world had literally crumbled around them. The town itself, now just an empty shell. There seemed no use in trying to make things better, it felt like a lost cause. George was nursing a warm beaker of water, pondering about the days that had followed the object's arrival. Jane was rightfully upset and depressed, she could not eat or drink anything and was unable to look at him or James. She felt let down by the world, felt like it was just this horrible, hating place. If there was such a thing as God then why did he not save them from all this. They did ponder the possibility that this was all a big plan, that it was all supposed to happen for a reason. James wondered why they were the only ones who were surviving in this unforgiving situation. The whole world was now nothing more than a barren wasteland, filled with unused office blocks and unloved landmarks. They felt like slaves to the light in the sky, it was their master. They were its experiment, like germs under a microscope.

George and Jane both wondered whether they should count themselves lucky for still being here. But it was difficult to believe that luck was linked to any of it, it was lonely. No one else around. All ties with the world had been cut.

Father Michael sat still in the church, praying, hoping. No answers came to him. It felt so strange, his faith had never let him down. At this time of need, there were no signs to help him. He cried. He could not help the tears rolling down his face and felt ashamed, useless and helpless.

Father Michael got up and walked towards the front doors. He opened them letting in the heat from the day run through his bones. The air was warm, the temperature was rising. Walking down the path in the courtyard, he took a sideways glance at the old oak tree, it still had hints of life, it looked sinister in its twisted shape. The grave stones underneath had remnants of bird droppings, but the birds along with everything else had... gone. The air was silent, nothing could be heard, except the wind. That haunting wind, making its way round the courtyard fences, around the branches in the trees. It echoed in his mind. It sounded almost like someone was calling for him, calling for his help. So he opened the old rusty gate to investigate and walked out onto the main street, turned and made his way to the edge of the town and kept walking along the path, while always looking left and right, hoping to see somebody...anybody. Nobody was there. He thought about the last few days, all the emotions he had felt in such a small space of time. The relief he felt when that scared couple and Mrs. Peterson walked into his church, how alone he felt when they all left abruptly.

Father Michael carried on his lonely journey, following the sound of someone who was calling him. Always checking, he looked into every house he passed, no sign of life. If he saw someone, something, it might give him hope. But still nothing could be seen. He continued to hear the voice calling, it sounded like a child, a girl.

Father Michael held out hope that maybe there were others here. Maybe there were, too scared to leave their houses.

Was that a curtain moving? He thought to himself. Walking over to investigate, it must have been his imagination playing with his mind. For a moment there he felt a flicker of hope, it did not last when he discovered nothing, but the voice he heard persisted in his brain. Feeling depressed, scared and afraid. More afraid then he ever felt before in his whole life. He wanted to find where the ghostly voice was coming from.

A thought occurred to him.

Was I sent here for this reason? Maybe it is my job to protect what remains here and guide it through this devastation.

He carried on. The breeze was coming thick and fast, but the breeze was humid. The sun beat down on his face and body, so hot that his legs could go no further. Out of breath, he walked up to a nearby house and knocked on the door, knowing there was going to be no answer. He then walked around to the back garden and looked through the kitchen window. He tried the back door, to his surprise it was unlocked, so he walked in. Feeling weird, he helped himself to a glass of water. He kept thinking about what the family was like who lived here. There were a few framed pictures dotted around and could feel a connection with them, he felt sad. On the kitchen window sill there stood a statue of a heart, engraved was the words *"I Love You, Mum"*. They were now gone, gone like everyone else. He sat down for a minute or so and thought,

Where is that voice coming from? He managed to gain some energy, he thought some more and drank a little, repeating this routine a few times over, then got up, ready to continue his search.

Walking back to the main road, Father Michael continued on the path to the town line. He reached it soon after. Stopping, he looked out at the devastation caused by the light. He looked up and could see it, looking down on him. Out in the distance he could see something looking at him, calling for him. *Was this the person who was calling out for me?*

He took a couple of steps and then the heat hit him. He could feel the water being evaporated from his body. It was much hotter than the last time he had crossed the line. Instantly, he was dehydrated and found it hard to breathe. Every time he took a breath, Father Michael got a lung full of hot air. He looked up again and the figure in the distance was still there, appearing to walk away from him.

He walked with as much speed as he could, almost a jog. He called out to the distant figure. They did not stop though, they seemed to still be moving away from him.

The heat he felt after jogging felt so extreme. He looked along the road to where he'd just been. The heat was rising from the road and pavements. He walked further into destruction and just kept going, trying to catch up with the ominous shape in the distance. The further into the destruction he went, the more it seemed like hell on earth. The heat was so intense. Plants, trees and animals were now just shadows of their former selves. Knowing he couldn't go any further as his legs were giving up, he halted.

Turning his head, he faced the town he had called home for such a long time and stared, he understood it was too far to return.

Looking towards the town, all looked luscious and green, it felt like an illusion, a paradise. The trees and grass were full of life, the houses in view looked perfect, it looked like a fantasy. That was his last memory of the town. The heat was starting to boil his blood. The pain of the burns, was unlike anything he had experienced before. He could see the flesh curling before his very eyes. The robes he had worn for many years at the church, suddenly combusted into flames. He was now in what felt like a furnace. His whole body engulfed in an inferno. Though he did not scream and did not shriek, the only thing to do was close his eyes and sacrifice himself. He prayed for the Petersons and hoped that God would be with them till the end and prayed for anyone else that may be alive, also for the being that had lured him out of town. He prayed for himself.

Father Michael was gone.

At the Petersons house they were still in

silence. George was still sipping his water and Jane was nibbling at a stale cracker, heaving after every bite she took. James was rocking on his chair, racking his brain on what to do to help. They were still sat around the kitchen table, when something happened, something that they were not expecting.

Chapter 13

A knock at the door, it echoed through the house. Jane and George jumped a little at the sound. They both looked at each other. James looked toward the door, there were shadows coming from the other side.

Jane stood up and moved carefully and nervously towards the door. Another knock occurred, making her jump again. She reached it and could hear the faint sound of people talking outside. Looking through the peephole, she saw that it was the Jones', who lived on the other side of town.

Jane opened the door, the warm air intruded the house and hugged Jane instantly. Sharon and Alex Jones were both staring at her, both looked surprised that they were there. Jane was too shocked to say anything, she just stared at them. George came up behind his wife and the four Merryville residents just hugged. James came to investigate, then went up to his bedroom.

Jane and George seemed unaware of James' departure. Tears were rolling down all their faces and they just stood this way for a while. All of them, unable to believe that there were others in town.

Sharon held Jane tight with her skinny arms. She was wearing a grey tracksuit. Jane remembered, before the disaster she always wore stunning outfits. She would have not worn a single strand of her blond hair out of place, she always had looked "picture perfect". She pulled away from Jane and stared at her with big hazel eyes. Jane could see that her appearance was now a complete contradiction to that "picture perfect" look, she was just like anyone else you could have met on the street. Jane could not believe that it was the same Sharon she had known.

Her husband, Alex, was a similar likeness. Before the disaster, a "perfect" businessman who had everything going for him, he was on the top of his game. He now donned a messy grey hair style and a similar tracksuit vest combo as his better half.

'I thought we were alone in town, you cannot know how relieved I am to see you,' Sharon said, breaking the silence.

'I feel the same, Sharon,' said Jane.

'We have some news on... that thing,' she pointed up at the sky. 'May we come in, I think it would be more appropriate.'

'Absolutely,' Jane lead the way into the kitchen. They all sat around the table, the Petersons were eager to hear the news they had. Pouring the last of their bottled water into some small glasses George joined the others at the table. James sat listening on the stairs, curious to what they had to say.

'We haven't done much since that thing came, it all seems so... so hazy. I feel like I'm in a dream and I'm going to wake up soon, but then that's wishful thinking,' Jane said.

'We felt the same, we literally were watching the world burn and crumble around us, we feel so helpless that we cannot do anything. But, Alex may have found a clue to what that thing is,' Sharon said. She turned to her husband. 'Tell them Alex. Tell them what you saw.'

Alex took a sip of the lukewarm beverage, then breathed heavy, like a chain smoker. He began.

'As you know we both were here the night that the light came closer and closer. We, like everyone else, did not know what it was. We're still unsure about what it is exactly. When everyone started to leave that night, so did we.'

'We drove back to our house and stood outside our front door looking up at the light in the sky. It shone so bright, as it still does now. Worried, like everyone else was, we came up with our own theories. We thought maybe aliens. But as time went on, thought maybe not. We saw what the light was doing to the world outside of the town and decided to stay put. We had not heard from any of the family. As you know we have no children, so that was at least something. We were worried and still are about our parents. They are in nursing homes up north. We had to assume that they could make the best decisions. We did try and call but the signal was limited and the phone line crackled and then cut out, the phone line on Landyard road was never a strong point to begin with.'

'The next day, we went to look around the town and came across Father Michael, who was in the church, no one else was around. I can see by the look on your faces that this is not news to you. Talking to him, he was saying that the night the light came down he called some of his contacts in other parts of the country, other parts of the world also. He told us that the temperature was becoming increasingly high, with some parts even catching fire.'

'We went back to our house and did not know what else to do. We cried, like many people would of. I felt so helpless. After ten years smoke free, I lit my first cigarette that night.'

'Feeling very reminiscent, Sharon decided to

get some photographs down from the attic in the house. Whilst looking around we found an old telescope. It was a good one, when it came out, it was powerful. We brought this down and set it up, wiped away the dust of many years from it, then looked through the lens and tried to find the light in the sky. I focused the dials to catch a clear picture of it.'

'What I saw was very intriguing. The shape of that thing is a half sphere. Patterned on it is a series of semi-circles. It is hard to explain really. The telescope does not take pictures, but I drew it and we wanted your James to have a look at it, if he is still into his science, space thing.'

He presented a piece of paper with the sketch on it, as Alex had described it was a half ball shape with semi-circles on it.

'An eye,' James said from the door way. He made the Jones and his parents jump with fright. 'It looks like half an eye,' he said. The four adults looked again at the sketch. It did indeed look like half an eyeball. It was a good way to explain what it looked like.

'Have you seen anything like this before, maybe in a magazine?' Sharon asked.

'No, but I have been watching it through my own telescope. I did not want to say anything until I knew what it was, but you have beaten me to the punch,' he replied.

'Does anyone actually know what it is doing here or what we can do?' Jane asked. No one said anything, the slight breeze in the air passed through the house.

'Well, as we cannot leave town, we need to think of something. I suppose only time will tell what it is here for,' said James. The five known remaining residents of the town were all sat in silence. They did not say anything, but were all thinking about what they could do.

'We need a plan, but as James said, we cannot leave town. We are, at the moment, safe in town. I suppose we just need to come together and figure this thing out,' George said. Everyone nodded in agreement, but each wondering if there was anything they could do.

George looked out of the kitchen window and saw that the sky was getting dark. There were a few clouds floating by overhead. The last of the sunlight sent shots of red and pink through them. Everything stood still. Silent.

Dear Diary,

Following my last entry, I have been trying to figure all this dream stuff out. I have been racking my brain about what it could be. I am still tired and at the moment I feel that I will be tired forever. I am in bed, even now. I feel too weak to move anywhere. I feel too tired to even write, but I want to record anything and everything.

Something came to me last night, I have no idea what it was. I do not know if it was a human or an animal, maybe even an object. It spoke to me, in the same voice I have been hearing for a while now. It told me to go to sleep. It told me that everything was OK. It told me that it would all be over soon.

I feel very skeptical. I remember reading somewhere, that if you stay awake for long enough then strange things happen to your brain and eyes. This, though, seemed so real. I could almost feel the words moving towards me. I asked who it was, or what it was. There was no reply. It stood there staring at me, I could feel the weight of its eyes. It was unnerving, I could feel myself becoming rattled. I closed my eyes and counted to ten... it was gone.

I laughed to myself, I felt even crazier than I did before. There was nothing standing there now, I was talking to an empty room. I still have a massive headache, unchanged from that day, when the light came. Why is all this happening to me? I hate it. I just want to know what is going on with me, the light in the sky and how to help. The shocking pain in my body reminds me that I am awake. I need to try and figure out what to do. I still feel like the control over my body is leaving me, every day I feel a little hazier and a little more distant.

I am so glad I have these pages to write on. It helps me, to at least try, to figure all this out.

Until next time...

Chapter 14

It was day four under the light. Sharon was feeling restless the night they came back from the Petersons house. She sat in silence in the living room. There was no electricity, no lights. The backup generator had ran out of fuel.

It's only a matter of time before the food goes bad, she thought. She walked to the kitchen and opened the refrigerator door... warm already inside.

She could feel herself welling up and could feel her stomach begin to ache, the feeling of acid travelling up her body was stinging her insides. There was a sickly feeling at the back of her throat, it stung as she tried to swallow. Knowing that she was going to be sick, she assumed the position hunched over the sink. She cried. Cried, not because of the food, but of everything since the devastation of the arrival. She cried because of the lack of control, for all those helpless people who had died. All of the families, including her own who are now potentially dead. Thinking about her parents, helpless in that nursing home, she thought that maybe they had been abandoned. She tried to push it from her mind, but the thought reared its ugly head each time she tried.

The whole house was so quiet, intimidating almost. She felt secluded, like a dream, looking in through a bubble at the world around her.

She resumed her place on the sofa in the lounge. It was dark everywhere except what caught the rays of the light from the shape in the sky.

It's not just a shape, it's an eye, reminding herself. She sat motionless for a while, not thinking about anything in particular, just listening to her breathing.

Wandering over to a big bay window in the living room, she looked up at it, looking down on the town. She began to shiver all over. She hugged herself with her thin pale arms. A tear escaped her eye and travelled the length of her face. She tried to think of something to help the situation, but could not.

'This is our life now,' she said to the empty house. She heard the floorboard creaking overhead. Alex. He was awake. The clock on the mantle said five thirty in the morning. The sun was slowly beginning to turn the sky pale.

She hastily went to the bathroom to grab some tissues, wanting to mask her tears as quickly as possible. Her eyes felt puffy from lack of sleep, stress…everything.

Now is not the time to breakdown, she told herself.

Alex descended the stairs and Sharon waited on the landing to greet him.

She just about managed to smile when he was at her eye level.

'Have you been crying again? I know it's difficult but at least we have each other,' he said.

'I know, it's just that I don't even know if the family are ok, we may never know,' she said solemnly.

'Look, I know it's difficult, I'm finding it difficult as well. It is a big change. We need to find a way to get through this, like we always find a way. We need to have some hope. If we don't have hope, we may as well leave town and be done with it. I feel the same Sharon, I could just cry and cry,' he explained. She stared at him for a moment and then held Alex in a tight embrace. She felt like she could stay this way forever, never letting go. It was nice, Sharon felt safe.

'Look at me,' he said, breaking the hug. 'I will not let anything happen to you, where you go, I go. Both of us will figure this thing out,' he promised. Walking into the kitchen, he grabbed their remaining juice from the now warm fridge. Sharon stayed in the hallway for a while longer, then assumed the position back at the window.

The light shone down on the remaining countryside. There was a definite line which was appearing where the town ended and the next began. One side was green and luscious and the other was burned and lifeless. It reminded her of the theatre masks, contradicting each other. One side happy and the other sad.

Alex sat in the kitchen, drinking his warm glass of juice. He winced at how bitter it tasted. Looking out of the kitchen window, the view was of an endless blue sky. Not a cloud to spoil the sight. He reminisced about times before all this, before the arrival, when both him and Sharon would have gone away for the day, to the beach maybe. He used to take Sharon out a lot. He thought about those memories, they all seemed so distant, so far away now. A different life. Deep in thought. He tried to be strong for Sharon's sake, though the situation was breaking him apart inside. Knowing how fragile Sharon could be, he kept telling himself that he needed to stay strong, to get both of them through this.

A terrible sensation suddenly overcame him. A feeling that something was going to happen. A few seconds after it occurred, the ground beneath his feet began to vibrate slightly. It made the remnants of juice in his cup ripple, like when someone drops a stone in a still lake. It rippled out, then began a new wave. The vibrations continued.

'Sharon,' he called. She was already at his side as soon as he called. They both crawled on the ground until they were under the table. The earth started to shudder more vigorously. Glasses were shaken from their positions on the work counters and broke as they hit the black and white kitchen tiles. It felt like a major earthquake, it grew and grew. The pulsing of the floor started to become a little unbearable. Sharon was screaming, while Alex held her close to his heart. There was a loud rumble, like a gigantic roar of thunder. It continued for what seemed like a lifetime, seeming like it was never going to stop. There was a high pitched ringing in both their heads.

Just as suddenly as it had started, it ceased.

They looked at each other. Both were sat motionless, in complete fear for their lives. They continued to hold one another and held each other tighter and closer than ever before.

Chapter 15

James was in his room franticly looking through his space magazines and books. He was searching for the mysterious half eye which hovered above them, even a mention of the eye would do, but there was nothing. His gut told him he would not be able to find anything before this venture started, as he had read them all so many times. The pages of the books were faded in the corners, worn down by years of reading them. But he thought that maybe, just maybe, he had missed something. Something important.

Looking at the eye through his telescope, it had not moved since the day it arrived, never changing or turning on any axis that he could see. It was just a static thing lurking over them.

Downstairs, the faint sound of his mother crying could be heard. He felt deeply depressed at that sound and wished there was something he could do to help everyone. He knew that he was at a lost cause with the whole thing.

His father, George, was out gathering some food and supplies from different places. Stocking up as much as they could. Without electricity, the food supply was limited. They had to gather mostly dry foods which required no special attention or storage. They would need to ration out what remained. Although at that moment in time there was a lot of dried goods, George did not know how long they would be stuck in this predicament.

He looked around at his bed, littered with various magazines. He packed them away into their drawer. Forgetting himself, tried the PC and then hit it when he realised what he had just done. Turning his chair towards the window he looked up at the eye once again, there was something almost mesmerising about it, he could not seem to look away from its gaze. There was also something dark, fearful and final about it.

The sound of his mother's crying pulled him back and he walked tentatively downstairs. The kitchen was empty and so he wandered into the lounge. His mother lay asleep on the sofa. James studied her and noticed how exhausted she looked. Her eyes were puffy and dark underneath. James noticed that there were more lines in her face since this had begun.

She must have cried so much she fell asleep, he thought to himself. He felt an urge to cry himself, at the sight of his mother laying there. She had always seemed so strong and confident, it was so out of character of her to breakdown so quickly. It broke his heart. He kissed her forehead and walked towards the patio doors, quietly unlocked the door and stepped outside into the warm, humid air. He looked skywards and fell into a daze. He could feel it looking at him. His digital watch said, 5:46am.

'How much longer are you going to keep us?' He asked it. There was no response... not at first.

What felt like a few hours passed, James glanced at his watch noticing that only a few seconds had. He could feel the short hairs on the back of his neck stand to attention. He felt very peculiar inside. Feeling a sense of urgency, he hurried back inside the house. His mum stirred on the sofa.

The ground began to beat fast but distant under foot. The ground shook the house, harder and harder. The vibration pulsed faster and the sound of objects falling over and glass breaking all over the house could be heard. It sounded like a window shattering and falling into a million pieces.

James ran to the sofa and they both held each other tightly. Jane embraced him protectively.

Then silence shadowed everything. Nothing could be heard anywhere at all. Their hearing felt like it had been muted.

His father hurried through the door only a few seconds later.

'Are you both OK?' He asked, looking concerned.

'I think so,' Jane replied, she looked down at James who looked more scared than ever before. James continued to hold his mother tight, even though it was over. He was shaking, his lips trembled with fear. A cold sweat came onto his brow, he wiped this away and began to catch his breath again.

'If you are both OK, then I think you better take a look outside,' he said mysteriously. Both Jane and James stood up from their position on the sofa, with legs like jelly, they reluctantly walked towards the doors. Astonishment and fear hit their faces when they looked up. The half eye had travelled considerably closer to the grounds surface. They all stood in silence and interest to see if it would move even closer, it didn't. Now it had got closer the feeling of complete helplessness became more real. It was so close, it seemed to be in reaching distance. It was so big, there was a strange sound, one of a strong wind.

It was huge, absolutely monstrous. The light that radiated off of its surface seemed to have dimmed on its descent, but was still extremely prominent. The detailing of the shape became much more apparent and distinctive. It was like James was looking at it through his telescope.

The Petersons were all completely shocked by it, they were too scared to scream, talk or even cry. They all felt that now the half eye was just too close for comfort.

Chapter 16

Dear Diary,

About three weeks has now gone by, since the light in the sky arrived. I have not been consistent in these diary entries, but not much more has happened. I have finally stopped falling asleep and waking up somewhere else. I am hoping that it is not going to happen again. However I have noticed, that since the light descended closer that the voices in my head are more prominent. They ask me questions, about life and about death. I'm sure that it is not my own voice which I am hearing. The voices change now and again, like someone else is interviewing me.

I am still scared to leave the house, but I may have to soon. My food is running low and the water from the tap is coming out dirty. I feel so unclean. I still feel like I have no control. I feel like at any moment I could just collapse. The dreams are consistent, every night. They come to me and talk to me in the cold and dark room. They ask me how I am feeling. It is the same conversation every night. I still have no idea what these people look like, as it is always dark. When I dream of this place, it feels so real. I feel the coldness of the chair I am lying on, the sound of the dripping pipes echo through my ears.

I was watching from my lounge window, the night that the light fell closer. I remember I felt like... that was it. That I was doomed. I knelt on the floor and prayed to every God I could think of. Although I am tired and I feel scared all the time, I am not ready to go yet. I have spent my days walking from one room to another. I try not to sleep, the fear of waking up in that cold, dark room is haunting. I keep thinking I see things that are not there. I see figures as the sun sets. They are standing around me, I feel it. I don't think the dreams...are really dreams. They are coming *for me in real life.*

I am losing my head. I will try and keep it together just a bit longer to see if these feelings go. My headaches have eased a little, but every time I wake up from a dream it is pounding once again. It always feels like my brain is about to explode.

There is not much else to say. I will write again when I have the energy. It is three in the afternoon, I'm going to try and sleep. The dreams don't haunt me so much in the light of day.

Until next time...

The air was mild and the sky was dark. Guarded by the object in the sky the town was now becoming cooler. Merryville was in a constant shade from the sun. The plants and trees in town has started to wilt due to the lack of sunlight and rainfall. With the electrical grid now not functioning, there was a bad smell in the air, mouldy food from warm fridges. There were a few bugs which circled the smell of their banquets. The water that came from the taps was now cloudy and unclean. They scavenged every day to find bottled water, they had already gathered what they could from the stores. They resorted to breaking and entering their neighbours homes.

Landyard Road, where the Jones' lived looked unspoilt, apart from maybe the flowers and greenery dying slowly. If someone looked at the road in a photograph there was nothing out of the ordinary. Sandydown Lane, where the Petersons lived would show a similar picture also.

As the days went on and turned to weeks, the two families became closer all the time. They shared what they could to get by, continuously thinking about what they could do to get out of this predicament. They thought of plans both realistic and not, nothing could be done. They were feeling low, their lowest yet. It seemed that this would be their lives from now on. A depressing and possible realistic thought.

They had looked at the floating apparition in the sky so much, when they closed their eyes to sleep they could still see it there. Haunting.

Chapter 17

'I got it,' George said. They all stared at him, looking skeptical. 'How far do you think that thing is away from us?' He asked.

'I don't know, maybe a mile, maybe a bit less,' Alex replied. They all become more interested. 'What are you thinking of George?' Alex wondered.

'I think it is a long shot, maybe we could scare it away. It might be too far away but I wonder if we could threaten it with something, maybe it will go away and leave the world alone,' he explained.

'What do you suggest we use, we have thought of everything,' Jane stated.

'Not everything. I was thinking maybe use something that is loud and bright... fireworks. I saw some at the store in the back room when we went looking around that day a couple of weeks ago. I didn't remember them till now. It must be old stock or something left over from the New Year. I suppose I didn't think that they would be important.'

'It's worth a try,' Alex agreed. He looked over to his wife Sharon who had been silent through all the conversations taking place at table. 'What do you think Shar?' He asked.

'What? yeah, try it. Anything to get rid of that thing,' she agreed. Her mind drifted elsewhere. Staring out of the Peterson's kitchen window, Jane looked in her direction and saw that her eyes were filling with tears. She held her hand under the table and gave it a big squeeze, for comfort. She looked at Jane and just smiled, then turned to look out of the window.

The Petersons house stood very still and quiet. Not an awkward silence, just a nice silence. Everyone was deep in thought. James was not around, he had gone out with the hope of finding something to help, clean water and food supplies. Down to the last few bottles, water was a rarity, like gold dust.

The day drifted by. George and Alex decided to use what fuel they had left in the cars to fetch the fireworks. Jane stayed behind with Sharon. James returned empty handed. They all moved to the lounge to sit down. The town around them was beginning to get dark as night crept towards them. The sun was making its final descent for the day and soon the moon would show its light. Although the chance of seeing the moon was minimal, there were a whole lot of clouds scattered around in the sky, not to mention the light which emanated from the half eye floating there.

As the sun set further, the sky turned an unusual, vibrant pink orangey colour. It reminded Jane of the night that the star which shone brightly became the end of the world as they knew it. It had the same colours and textures. She felt overwhelmed at the sight of all those clouds mixing together. It was a big spectrum of light and dark shadows, twisting around in the sky.

Jane recalled how nice that last "normal" evening had been. How perfect it was. All of the guests enjoying themselves, eating and chatting. She remembered Mrs. White coming up to her and talking about her Wendy and also seeing the Robinstons. She recalled scanning the party scene and seeing all the happy faces, only moments before the arrival, then all their faces after the arrival, a complete conflicting picture. So many scared faces, it was pure terror. Sure, she was feeling the same, it was a bizarre night. One that ruined so many lives, in such a short space of time.

She drifted off into many thoughts in such little time. When she rejoined the present day, the sky was darker, a deep blood red. The sight of some stars twinkled up ahead, although this view was obstructed by the evil hanging over them. Jane stood and started turning on their light source, battery powered nightlights.

'I wonder how long the boys are going to be,' Sharon wondered. Jane could hear the worry in her voice.

'I'm sure that they will be here soon,' Jane replied. She turned to James. 'No luck with finding any water today?' she asked.

'Nope, the whole town seems completely dry, I'll have a look in the pub tomorrow and see if they have any left. I wouldn't get your hopes up though. They might have some fizzy drinks or something like that,' he replied. It went quiet.

Sharon looked as though she was about to cry. Maybe she thought that this was the end of them as well. She looked like she was about to say something important, then the front door opened. George and Alex walked in together carrying an armful of rockets each.

'Wow, I thought we only needed one,' Jane said looking at George.

'Well I thought that we might as well give ourselves a show, even if I doesn't work. What else is there to do?'

'Shall we get started?' Jane asked.

'May as well, no time like the present.'

Chapter 18

Jane looked at her watch, a routine lost in recent times, 6:17pm. The sky was growing darker and it was nearly time to begin the display. George and Alex were setting up the spectacle out in the Petersons back garden. Jane felt a sense of excitement, she was unsure why, but she did. Looking over at Sharon, who looked nervous, she didn't quite look like she was here, more of a ghost in another time. Jane observed her from the corner of her eye, she looked old, drained and haggard. She wondered if she herself looked the same, Jane hadn't looked into the mirror for what seemed like forever.

James was outside helping his father. It made Jane smile. She stood from her seat and walked over the window to observe the men at work.

'What if this doesn't work?' Sharon asked.

'It has to, we have nothing else,' Jane replied.

'What if the reaction it gives isn't the one we want, maybe it will start a war. I'm so scared Jane. I don't want to live like this anymore, in fear and isolation. I want to be with my family.'

'I'm sure it will work. I'm sure your family had sense to take cover underground or something. They will be waiting for you.' Jane walked towards Sharon and sat beside her. She put her arm around her and they both felt the comfort and the intimacy between them gave them hope.

'Listen, if it doesn't work, at least we have one another. I know that's not the best outcome, but at least it's something. There is nothing else to do, we can't leave town, we will be burned alive.' Sharon did not reply, she just nodded and tears began to escape her eyes.

She glanced at her watch again, 6:38pm. Jane began to feel herself becoming nervous. Not necessarily in a bad way but in a "I hope this works" way. They all hoped it would. The fireworks had been set up. George and Alex were walking towards the house again, James following behind.

'All ready?' She asked.

'I think so, do we still have those beers from the BBQ somewhere?' George said.

'I think there maybe a few in the pantry, right at the back. I'll come with you.' Jane and George walked into the kitchen. Alex was holding his wife close on the sofa, she was still scared and upset by the whole plan.

George opened the pantry door and walking in a step to turn on the small battery powered light which swung overhead slightly. He was saddened by the lack of food that he saw, never had the cupboard been so empty. A few bean cans stood there and a few fruit salads were scattered about. He saw the cans of beer glistening in the light. He reached over and grabbed them.

'Do you think this is going to work?' Jane asked.

'I have no idea hun, I hope so. It will go one of three ways.'

'Three?'

George nodded at this.

'One, our plan will work and it will leave us alone. Two, it will go the opposite and attack us in defense. Three, nothing will happen. But whatever does happen, I love you.'

'I love you, too.' She hugged him for a while. They could hear Sharon crying slightly from the lounge. James and Alex were comforting her and assuring her that everything will be alright. Jane hoped for everyone's sake that they were right.

The time was 6:53pm. The Jones and the Petersons were outside in the cool air. George and Alex walked towards the fireworks with a box of matches in hand. Sharon had got herself under control, Jane put her arm around her for comfort. Jane felt her palms go moist. James was more excited about the free firework display. It seems like a lifetime ago that anything exciting had happened, in a way it was that long ago. They were becoming used to the fact that their supplies were limited. Jane wished she could be so enthusiastic about it all, but she could feel doubt travelling through her body, especially since her conversation with Sharon.

6:56pm, a spark was shining from the first firework lit. A few seconds passed, then silence. A swoosh or air forced the rocket skywards and it exploded into a spectrum of brightly coloured sparks. It was so beautiful. There was a pause, they all looked skywards, even after the rocket. Nothing happened. Sharon started to cry and went inside the house again. Jane could feel the disappointment engulfing her body.

Another rocket went skywards. The same outcome.

'Maybe try lighting them all at the same time,' Jane called over to them. George put a thumbs up to this. Alex grabbed his own match and struck it on the side of the box, then both men started frantically lighting all the fireworks as fast as they could. They tried to light as many as they could before they all started to explode into life.

They both stood back just in time, the first one flew up into the air and was followed by a succession of many others, one after another. Rockets and fountains lit the sky. Jane looked up, feeling hopeful, she held James in her arms. As the first one exploded it began a loud series of bangs and pops. It was the loudest thing any of them heard. James covered his ears but continued to watch. Jane looked at all the colours dancing in the sky. Blues, greens, reds, the list of colours were endless. The display shook the ground underfoot, it was over in seconds.

The silence, that followed the loud bangs, seemed too quiet. There was a pause, nothing happened. They all felt defeated. George and Alex shrugged their shoulders and walked towards Jane and James.

Suddenly there was a loud noise, which pierced the silence. It was an unexpected noise and made all of them jump, Jane let out a scream. She knew where the noise was coming from and looked up towards the sky and watched in anticipation at what might happen. They all were standing outside on the patio area and braced themselves.

At this point, anything could happen.

Chapter 19

Dear Diary,

I have just had the shock of my life. It was quiet in the house, then all of a sudden there were loud noises coming north of here. Coming from the Petersons place I presume, as they are the only ones I have seen still in town. Maybe there are others around. I hope so. It is a sad thought that everyone blindly went into the scorching heat and burned on the way to their final destination.

I looked out of the highest window in the house and could see there were fireworks being let off. I stayed and watched for a while. All the colours were so beautiful. I could see that a big cloud of smoke was rising from the bright colours. It rose up to the light in the sky.

After a few seconds the fireworks stopped

and the cloud of smoke rose higher. I saw it hit the light that had been threatening us for such a long time. I was shocked and frightened at the noise I heard next. The noise that came from the light. It cut through the air like a knife. It went quiet for a few moments...

Nothing could be heard anywhere. Anticipation filled the air. The Petersons and the Jones all stood in a line outside the Petersons residence. They all looked towards the sky... waiting. The sound came flying through the air again. It sounded like an animal screaming in pain, a bear in a spike trap. It continued. It was distressing. There was a brief interlude again and then the sky started to change.

The hovering half eye in the sky began to change the colour of its white light and began to turn a pink. The colour continued to change until it was a postbox red colour, then darker. A huge wind blasted the onlookers, there was something malicious about it. The wind continued, it was like being stood in front of an immense industrial fan. They all felt as if they could be knocked over by the force.

Time passed and the gushing force calmed. There was again a silence. The light which radiated off of it now made everything a rose colour. It felt like a dream, when something was not quite right.

'What is happening?' Sharon struggled through tears. No one answered her cry. They were all hypnotised by what was happening in front of their eyes. The wind began to start again and this time the half eye in the sky fell from its position in the sky to the earth below. It made a bang ten times louder than that of the fireworks, the vibration was so severe that it jolted everything out of its place. All of the onlookers fell to the now broken paving stones. The sound vibrated through the ground and shattered many windows as the sound waves travelled. The sound of breaking glass echoed, they were now trapped for sure. No one said anything.

Looking behind, Jane saw that the windows were cracked and the walls to the house were breaking down. Dust from the bricks and from the roof crumbled down and fell upon their heads. They all moved away from the house, scared that at any moment the house would collapse.

They reverted their attention to the thing that now surrounded the town entirely. In the distance they could hear a car alarm going off. A car which someone had left to leave town, or was there someone else? The question came into all their heads, then the car alarm stopped. Silence reawakened.

'What the hell just happened?' Sharon asked again.

'I have no idea, I think the fireworks made it a whole lot worse,' Alex replied. 'We can't even leave town now, not that we would. Now we have no choice. This is terrible.'

'Calm down, maybe something else will happen, I don't know. We need to keep calm though, shouting won't help us,' Jane said. She looked at George, hoping to get a plan from him. He just stood silent.

'What shall we do now?' Alex asked.

'Wait. There is nothing else to do. We need to wait. I don't think it will be long before something happens, I think the fireworks have put some wheels in motion,' George concluded.

A little time went past, maybe a minute, maybe an hour. The two families stood where they were for a while, then cautiously went back inside the crumbled walls of the house.

They immediately noticed that all the interior decor had been smashed and broken from the impact. There was glass and china covering the floor, it looked like a bomb had exploded. They all collapsed on the sofas and thought about their next move.

Jane held James tight in her arms, whilst George held them both. Sharon and Alex were sobbing to each other on the other couch. It was deeply depressing and they all felt like this was the end of everything.

... I was jolted from my position and fell down. I hit my head on the edge of a chair. It did not seem to hurt, not as much as the headache I already have. I seemed to be unable to move for a few seconds, maybe it was a few minutes. When I did eventually get back up and found my balance, I thought my eyes were going weird. Everything was a pink colour.

I looked out over the town, which I had called home for so many years and it was shadowed in a rosy pink blanket. I know it doesn't sound that bad, but it was. I looked up at the light, it had changed to a deep red colour.

When the shock of what happened settled, I noticed that my car alarm was sounding. I grabbed my keys as quickly as I could and silenced it. I continued to stare out of the window. There was nothing else to do, it was so surreal. I can hardly believe it now.

I could not move. My body ached all over. The headache seemed to deepen in my skull, it felt like my head was about to blow up like one of the fireworks. I sat on the chair which stood beside me. I thought about everything. It seemed so strange to think that just over three weeks ago, the world was fine. Now, it was the complete opposite. This was insane.

The voices in my head have let me be for now. I still feel that I am not in control of the decisions I make. I still feel like I am going completely insane.

Long ago, I remember my mother told me about a great, great auntie who used to live here, in Merryville. She had headaches, she heard voices. Her name was Shelly, she was locked in a mental asylum, considered a risk to society. She would rave night and day about these beings that were coming after her. She explained that in the night, the voices came. She saw shadows in her room at night. She talked about the end of the world, how it is not as far away as we all think. She had foreseen what literally had happened in Merryville in the past few weeks. Nowadays we would call these people mediums or psychics. She was labeled as crazy and too dangerous for normal society. I even thought she was crazy growing up. She sounded like a loon. But now that everything she has said had come true, I know she wasn't crazy at all. She was just blessed with the power to see the future, even though she probably did not think of it as blessed, rather cursed. I feel like I am going down the same spiral staircase as she did. All her symptoms were the same.

I need to rest a little, I feel my breathing becoming harder. I have a feeling I will be writing more before the night is over.

Until next time...

Chapter 20

The ground underfoot began to rumble slightly. Everyone was silent and motionless. The ground carried on its hum for a while, building until the vibration could be felt more prominently, continuing until it began to pulse more vigorous.

'Now what?' Sharon said, feeling like she could not take another hit. They all saw that she was breaking down in front of their eyes. The others may have felt the same way, but they were too numb to react in such a way.

They scrambled to the back patio doors to look outside, to see if anything was happening. There was not... not at first.

Then, after a while longer of the pulsing and vibration, the ground seemed to split. They all looked with wonder.

'What is that?' Jane asked, she was mainly asking herself, rather than anyone else.

'I have no idea, is the ground breaking up? I think it is,' George said.

The ground around the perimeter of the town continued to break and split in the same fashion. They all ran outside and towards the edge of town to investigate what was happening. As they got closer to the town line they noticed that the ground was beginning to lift. Continuing their journey to the edge of town and after about five minutes of constant running they reached it. Sure not to get to close to the thing that was keeping them prisoner, the Petersons and the Jones were watching the outside world. They thought that they were all losing their minds as they watched themselves depart the Earth.

The ground continued to rise, all they felt was the rumble of the ground beneath them.

'We're moving,' Jane said.

'Where to?' Sharon asked.

'I have not got a clue, what is happening?' Everyone continued to look at the platform that they were now on. The ground below them, dry and baron was becoming further away by the second, still they could not believe what was happening.

They were now a couple of metres away from the surface of the Earth. The object was carrying them up further now, with more speed. Before they knew it they were five metres, then ten.

They all looked down and the feeling was one of flying, like they were looking out of an airplane window at the ground below. James approached the line and touched the wall keeping them captive. Upon doing this, a gush of intense temperature coursed through him and he was pushed back towards the others. James promptly got up and rejoined his mother's side.

They were definitely separated from the ground now and floating sideways. They could see the space where the town should be below them. It looked like a crater. There was a half sphere shape, like a bowl, which had been left behind. They all looked at each other.

'Where are we going?' Sharon asked hysterically. Jane looked at her. She felt moved at how much this was affecting her, as it was everyone else.

'A new life,' Jane replied.

They were carried higher and further. Below they could see that the world was basically dead. It looked crumbled and dry. Maybe some people were still alive, but they could not know. They were being taken to another place. They could still see, in the distance, the hollow ground where Merryville had stood since the start of time. They continued their journey.

'What now?' George asked. No one replied. They just hugged each other, whilst still looking down at what used to be their home.

Dear Diary,

I guess we are going on a trip somewhere else. I can see that we are now floating through the air and the Earth is below us. I just hope that the pain and suffering is over now. I hope this thing we are travelling in is taking us to a new life. Somewhere safe. Somewhere with hope.

After the ground started to lift up I walked down the stairs and into the lounge. It was complete carnage after the light impacted the earth. All my earthly possessions were broken into a million bits on the floor. There was a photo that had fell from the shelf above. I turned it over and a smile was made on my face. It was the day Wendy and I went to the seaside. It must have been a good five years ago now.

I just stared at the photo, I hugged the photo and thought about where she might be now. I hope when I do pass from this life I will find out. I have missed her every day since she died, not a minute has gone past *that I haven't thought about her. She was going to go to medical school, which was before that careless driver ran her down. They never did find out who it was. I still forget sometimes that she has gone. I still speak about her to people, forgetting that she is now passed.*

I sat down, where I still sit now. I can see out of the window and see the stars. I wonder if one of the stars we have passed was Wendy. Shining brightly. I would like to think so.

I have come to the end of this diary. I am ready to put it on the shelf and open up a new book. To start a new chapter in my life. Thank you for being there for me at my times of need.

From your loyal writer, now and forever. Nora

Looking down at the dead planet below them, they all thought about the happy times they had had. There were so many questions still unanswered. They all wondered if anyone was still alive down there.

The further away they went, the earth got smaller and smaller. They looked above and saw endless sky and stars, as they were getting higher. Looking again at the Earth, it was now smaller than ever. They scanned all around them and were beginning to see stars go past them. They could see the whole solar system. They did not have any difficulties breathing, the atmosphere enclosed in the town remained the same.

The Earth got smaller still. They looked in the direction they were heading and saw endless black sky. It was frightening. Tears were rolling down all their faces.

They took one final look at their home planet and saw that it was so small now. Almost just a dot.

The Earth was now just an ENTITY.

Entity II

Prologue

Deep in the darkest parts of space, there is a light. A light that shines brighter than any star. It travels through the debris, rocks and remnants of space crafts, lost in time forever. Far in the distance, there is an entity. An out of place eye, leisurely floating through the zero gravity.

With the dark backdrop of infinite universes, the eye's radiance is even more powerful. It stands out, big and bold. Within the eye there is something. Something that does not fit out here in the endless black, a town.

The town of Merryville, trapped inside the vessel now travelling through space, illuminated by the bright dome which covers it. Quiet and isolated, it looks like a depressing and forgotten snow globe. The foliage dying and wilting. The buildings which are there, broken and crumbled.

The town church is nothing but a pile of rubble, it had been rocked to and fro with so much vibration, the steeple had collapsed onto the roof and the walls are now lying dead, in the graveyard with the deceased. The twisted tree outside, still stands proud, its roots firmly in the ground and its haunting, sinister look unchanged.

Across the street the local pub 'The Hill's Angel' now in shadow of the trees that did not make it. Broken glass litters the floor and the luscious garden planters once full of life, now dead and shriveled.

A similar scene played out across the town of Merryville. Though the towns that once surrounded this quiet community had a different fate.

One house in the town is occupied by several people. These are the remaining residents of Earth, now floating through the universe. The Petersons; George, Jane and James, along with the Jones'; Alex and Sharon. They are all sitting together, looking worried and confused. No one saying anything. What is there to say? In shock they remain vacant and still.

Across the town there is a noise coming from another little house, detached and alone. Nora White, sitting in her living room, looking through the window at the destruction outside. A tear escapes her eye and drips down onto the floor. She can see that beyond her house in the distance, the town she had called home for so many years is now a crumbled wasteland.

This is Merryville. This is life from now on.

The six survivors know that they need to find out what is behind all this, though they could never have braced themselves for what was to come.

Welcome to the Entity.

Chapter 1

'I wonder where we are going.' Jane said looking out into the darkness which was surrounding their travelling town. There was not much to see, there were a few stars, but they looked so far away. Now and again a rock cluster went by, this caused the ground to rumble slightly underfoot, similar to that of a plane going through a cloud.

'I have no idea,' George replied. 'It's starting to get cold, put this coat on,' he handed his wife a black jacket, which she took and slipped on as quickly as she could.

'Well, wherever it is, I just hope that it is better than the devastation we have just left,' she said, thinking back to their last few weeks on Earth. She remembered how the whole planet was burned and lifeless, it made her heart heavy as the sadness resurfaced. She also thought about all those people who had perished due to the light, which was now carrying them through the solar system. She snuggled in with George and James, both of whom were quiet and deep in thought about what might become of them.

James looked at both his parents with a sense of defeat. He was the one who was knowledgeable about science and the solar system, yet he failed to help. His emotions were high and deep down he wanted to cry, but knew that this would make his mother more upset, so he held it in.

Across the room sat Sharon and Alex, both looking puffy eyed with dried tears on their faces. There was nothing any of them could do to help the situation. They were helpless and had no control over anything. Alex and Sharon just held hands whilst looking up at the stars floating past.

They carried on travelling for what seemed like hours, maybe even days. No one spoke, there was nothing else to be said, no one knew anything. The cold from space was starting to set into all their bones. Their breath could be seen, misty, as they exhaled. Sharon and James were the first to start shivering with the drop in temperature, then the others followed shortly after. The air was like ice, daggers digging into their skin.

George and Alex decided they would both search for as many jumpers and blankets that they could find. They managed to get a few but nothing could block out the cold. George was concerned as he was sure that hypothermia would affect them all sooner or later. His mind wondered a little, he was trying to remember a documentary he saw a while ago about the effects of cold weather, but failed to come up with anything.

'Are we going to die out here?' James asked his dad, without emotion, as if it would be better that way.

'I hope not son. Just cover yourself with everything you can, hopefully we will be OK,' he replied, though he did not feel convinced himself. This answer did not give anyone any comfort, it just reminded everyone that they had no control over anything, not even the temperature. Back on Earth it was easy, they would just turn on a switch and it would heat the house up lovely, up here in space, they did not have that luxury. Jane noticed that James' lips were starting to go blue.

'What are we going to do George?' Jane asked. 'We are all freezing, James is changing colour. I do not know how much longer we can hold on here,' she added. He looked at her with sad eyes, knowing that what Jane was saying was true, he also didn't think they could hold on. George couldn't find the words to speak, he couldn't think, it was so cold. Jane could see by the way George was moving, that he was struggling too. She knew that he did not have any idea what to do. They had to get used to the fact that they were going to die out here in space, miles from anywhere, miles from home.

James got up and started upstairs, every now and then stopping to catch some energy. He managed to get to the top of what felt like a mountain and walked into his bedroom, grabbed some pillows and gingerly walked back to the stairs again. James descended the staircase and when he reached the lounge area again he covered his face to warm up his lips and nose.

They all looked towards the door which lead outside, there were icicles forming on the window. It formed on both the outside and the inside, they made it look like a broken pane of glass. Everyone still remained in silence. Jane and James were hugging each other. They could see that George was trying to think of a plan. Alex and Sharon were cuddling up under a few blankets and old bedsheets. All were shivering.

The minutes went past slower the colder it got. The Petersons and the Jones' were all trying to keep warm under their covers, they all believed that soon they would be dead. No one said anything much, James moaned involuntarily due to the cold. The cold was creeping into Georges joints, making them ache. They hurt like nothing he had ever felt before in his life. Feeling that he could cry it was so painful, he stood and walked around a little. Sharon had drifted off to sleep, or was it because of the cold? She was still breathing though, they could see her breath shoot from her mouth every now and then, though staggered and short.

'Can you hear that?' Jane asked.

'No, what?' George replied, he could see the concern on her face.

'I thought that I could hear something, like a rumbling sound.'

George just looked at her puzzled face then got up and walked towards the back patio doors to look outside. There didn't seem to be anything different. He opened the door and his breath was taken right from his lungs when the cold whipped at him, stepping out and closing the door to avoid the frosty air intruding too much more on the others. He walked out and stepped onto the grass. The grass, which was frozen, broke underfoot like twigs. The crunching sound it produced seemed so much louder than it really was, due to the deadly silence. He would never have thought that he would miss the simple sound of the birds singing or crickets calling.

George looked up at the sky, but didn't notice any change at first. He continued to look out into the endless black. The noise that Jane had mentioned before could now be heard. It was starting to become more prominent, though it seemed still far away. All the time the noise could be heard more clearly. There was a rumbling sound rising towards them all.

The ground began to pulse and in front of George, on the other side of the barrier surrounding the town appeared a huge eyeball. It stared down, looking directly at him. He felt uncomfortable and was sick with how scared he was. Jane joined him, but could not manage to look directly at the eye, darting around looking at them. The rumbling noise continued as they approached it. The town crept closer and closer and the fear rose higher in their bodies.

'Look Jane,' George said.

'I don't want to, it's looking right at us. I'm scared.'

'It's changing.'

Jane turned around and both of them looked. The eye that was a few seconds ago looking at them, started to split. It opened up like a clam. Their vessel was heading for the open space it had produced. They entered. It was even darker than before, which seemed impossible, but true.

All were scared about what could happen now. The temperature changed and it was starting to become warmer again. Their breath could no longer be seen, still they shivered, maybe with fright. George looked towards the other side of town and noticed that the place they had just entered was beginning to close behind them, like elevator doors. Soon they would lose the remaining light that shone on them from the stars. Even the light from the vessel they had been travelling in was no more.

It closed moments later and all the survivors of Merryville were sitting in complete darkness, not even the battery lights would work. They all just sat and awaited their fate.

∞

'This is fantastic, they have now arrived into the loading area. They all seem to be intact. No one died on the journey here, which is good. We can now begin the next phase of my plan. All that I have worked for comes down to these final few people. Wait here for my next instructions, we need to initiate phase two now.'

Chapter 2

The whole town was enveloped in darkness, everywhere they looked they saw black. They couldn't even see their hands in front of their faces. The cold was beginning to ease and the temperature was becoming more bearable, though it was still cold. They all felt slightly more hopeful that they might just survive this journey. Sharon finally stopped shaking and James returned to a normal body colour.

Nora was under her bed covers, warming up, when the room she was in became dimmer. Peeking out from behind the floral duvet, watching as the town got darker and darker until it was pitch black.

'What the hell is going on?' She asked herself. She felt the need to speak the words out loud, to see if it was real. It was. She pulled her feet around to the floor and stood up. Her head went dizzy with disorientation. Slowly and gingerly walking towards where her window was and tried as hard as she could to see something. There was nothing to see, just an endless shadow.

'What is happening?' Sharon asked. Nobody was listening, they were all deep in their thoughts. They were waiting for something else to happen. It was so quiet they could hear a pin drop. It was so silent that it rung loud in their ears, like a constant buzzing.

Seconds went by and turned to minutes, no one said anything. The stillness grew and grew.

There was a noise coming from somewhere. They could not pin point it. James thought that it was coming from behind them, Jane thought it was coming in front. The noise persisted. As it became louder it was more distinctive, it sounded like an alarm of some sort. Still it got louder and began vibrating in all their ears. There was no light and the town was still pitch black, but with the distraction of the alarm they did not seem to worry about it as much.

Nora was watching from her window at the time the alarm started to sound. From her high bedroom window she could see something glowing with the noise. It was red, it reminded her of a panic light she saw once in a hospital. Just one red light, small but prominent. If she wasn't watching from the top room it would not have been in sight. The alarm persisted and the red light was in sync with the noise it produced. On and off it went.

'I need to get to the Petersons house as soon as we get some light,' the voice inside her head agreed. She began to move towards her stairway, having lived here so long she knew the house like the back of her hand, though she felt uneasy in light of the situation, or no light as the case was. She felt for the top step and carefully, whilst holding the handrail, descended into what felt like a sea of dark below. Her body soon realised that it was becoming warmer by the second and she shed a layer of clothing. From down here the glow of the red light was no longer in sight. She could not see through the darkness that had invaded the town.

In the kitchen she felt around for the drawer, in which there was a torch. Clicking it on and off for some source of light, but there was none. She fumbled around with the battery compartment and when she opened it, water ran out. The water was produced by the cold they had felt only a few minutes earlier. A lot of items must have turned to ice and now that it was hotter they were thawing out. So she waited, waited in hope of some light, sooner rather than later.

The Petersons and the Jones' all walked in the

direction of the town line. They kept stopping, making sure that they were not going to walk into the barrier which surrounded their little town. As they got closer, they noticed a red colour emanating from somewhere unknown.

The alarm suddenly silenced and all that could be seen now was the constant glow from the red light. The air was quiet again with anticipation. All the residents of Merryville, watching and waiting. Jane turned towards the others and could see their faces were pink in the glow.

A little time went past and a loud sound occurred, like a horn. It was followed by the most haunting voice any of them had ever heard.

'Do not panic,' the voice said. 'We will shortly be sending you all to sleep, when you awake, you will be greeted by a host,' the voice added. The Petersons as well as the Jones all looked at each other, worried about what might be happening.

'What the hell is going on? Who was that?' Sharon asked.

'I have a feeling we will soon be finding out,' Jane replied. After the confusion set into all of them, a turbine started. It sounded like an airplane engine starting. After a few seconds, they all felt the spray of some kind of strong smelling chemical. It wasn't long until they started yawning, and soon became victim to the mysterious liquid.

Merryville had been put to sleep. As Nora closed her eyes she could just make out a light appearing up above. Silence was reawakened as they all fell into a dreamless sleep. Nora hoped that when they all woke up they would be somewhere nicer. Somewhere they could call home.

∞

'Phase two is complete. They are now all asleep. Press that button, it will start transporting the bodies to the ship. When they wake up, we will give them a little time to come to terms about what is happening, then I will signal the host to collect them. Oh, it is exhilarating, my life's work will soon be concluded. Now we play the waiting game.'

Chapter 3

The room was cold and damp. There was little light, it was illuminated by a single, lonely swinging bulb dangling from the ceiling. The way it moved was unnerving, watching it like a pendulum swinging away and then back again, it reminded James of a scene of a horror movie he had stayed up late to watch. The Petersons, the Jones' and Nora were all huddled together. Some still asleep.

James was the first to awaken from the chemical induced sleep. It took him a minute or two for his eyes to focus. The room was just a little too dark to see much. What could be seen was a silhouette of some sort of chair or table, sitting in the center of the room. It was quiet, he thought for a minute that he had gone deaf, then he heard something. The sound of a tap dripping. It came in at regular intervals. Beating out a steady rhythm. The noise put James on edge as he felt like he was on his own, the others were still asleep.

George, Alex and Sharon all woke up next.

They huddled closer, scared in their new surroundings.

A long time went by it seemed, Jane stirred from her deep comatose state and Nora did not seem to be breathing that well, her breath coming through short and husky.

'Where are we?' James asked his father. He knew that his father did not know, but asked the question all the same.

'I have no idea, it's cold though,' he replied. All of the conscious residents of Merryville daren't make a move, as fear of what might happen began to surface. Jane stirred more and her eyes started to flicker as she was waking up.

'Where are we?' Jane asked, just as James had. George gave the same, simple reply. She sat up and got her eyes focused on the light swinging carelessly in the middle of the room. All went deadly quiet again and she began to hear the sound of the dripping tap. That sound, invaded her ears. It was haunting, but was a constant reminder that they were still alive in this hell.

'This place, it seems so familiar. Almost like I have been here before,' she said. 'Are we still in town,' she added.

'I don't know, I just woke up here like you. I haven't looked around anywhere else,' George replied. 'How about you, Sharon. Alex. Any ideas?'

Both Sharon and Alex shook their heads, George could just make out their movement in the dim light.

Jane looked around and saw that Nora was sleeping beside her. Shocked, she let out a little breath and then got herself under control as she realised who it was.

'Nora?' She said. There was no reply, but Nora was becoming restless in her sleep. Jane shook her to try and wake her up. 'Nora' she said again.

The old woman had registered this and opened her eyes slowly. She was startled by seeing both the Petersons and the Jones' all by her side.

'Are you OK,' Sharon asked her.

'Yes dear, it's a little dark isn't it,' she said as she sat up. She herself looked around the room they were in and then her heart dropped inside her. The sound of the dripping tap rang in her ear like an echo. She knew exactly where she was, she had been here before. She had dreamt about this room since the eye came down and took their little town away. Nora began to panic and shake, though she was unsure why she felt like this. Concerned, the others gave her some space, but also tried to comfort her.

'I have been here. This room, that dripping tap. I have heard it in my dreams for weeks. I woke up from being here with a massive headache, the headache which grew over the following few weeks. I was visited by some people in this room who did something to me, I'm not sure what. I want to get out,' Nora explained, becoming unsettled.

After Nora's explanation, it soon became apparent why Jane had recognised it to. She too had been here, in a dream, she thought. She was grabbed by something, managing to break free from their grasp, she woke up in her living room. She recalled every second of the experience like it was yesterday.

'Something very strange is going on here, I do not like it one bit. Nora said that she had been here, well so have I and it was not pleasant. I was grabbed by someone, or something,' she replayed it over in her head again and with the realisation that it was not a dream at all, a little tear threatened in her eye. She knew that it seemed too real.

The others were just listening to Nora and Jane tell their stories. All of them were becoming more worried with every word said.

'How is that possible though, how did you get here and back?' Alex asked. Both Nora and Jane shrugged their shoulders in unison.

'I have no idea, after that first encounter I kept waking up all over the place. I thought I was losing my mind when I realised that the dreams were real,' Nora said. She looked around some more and just let her head fall to the floor where she had laid. 'I never thought that I would see this place again, I thought all that was over now.'

Some time went past, the dripping of the tap acted like a clock. A drip would occur every three seconds or so. A minute went past, then it must have been an hour. The light above their heads had stopped swinging so rapidly and was now just hanging down. As their eyes adjusted more they could make out the room a little better. There was a chair in the middle of the room, similar to a dentist chair. A chair that Nora knew very well from her encounters.

Drip.

Drop.

They seemed to be sat in the same place for hours. Nothing happened. None of them said anything for ages, they were all processing what was happening, also what could happen next. All were wondering where they were and what had happened to their town, their home.

Drip.

Drop.

'How long have we been here for?' Sharon asked.

'Couple hours I reckon,' Alex replied. They all let out a little sigh.

A few more minutes of deafness passed and

then something could be heard in the distance. Footsteps, coming closer. It seemed so loud after being so quiet for so long. A bolt lock sounded, making them all jump. Sharon let out a little scream as it did so.

All they could see was a brilliant white light, invading their eyes. Nothing else could be seen apart from the white. As their eyes started to adjust, they had little stars and shadows dancing around in front of them. Their eyes continued to focus more.

Two figures could be seen standing in the doorway.

Chapter 4

The two figures loomed in the doorway. It felt like everything was moving in slow motion to the residents of Merryville, though only a few moments had actually passed. The two silhouettes stepped forward towards them. Terror ran through their bodies and the panic was making them shake with fear and anxiety. Their eyes started to adjust to the blinding light, they could now see that a man and a woman were standing in front of them. The two were dressed in similar clothing and both had the same little logo on their polo tops, like they were wearing a uniform of some sort, though none of them recognised the picture.

    The woman looked about twenty or so and had short spiky hair, she had deep brown eyes, which looked almost black in the dull lighting. She had a thin build and was short. The man looked about the same age and looked like a bodybuilder, his arms were big and he was built like a brick wall. He had short hair also, as well as piercing green eyes that seemed to have the ability of looking right through you.

'Don't worry,' the man said. 'We are here to help,' he continued. The residents of Merryville looked at each other, quizzical about if he was telling the truth.

'Where are we?' George asked. 'Did you put us in here?' He felt like he could ask a thousand questions in the same breath. It was visible on all their faces that they were scared. Though the newcomers were prepared for the questions. It was an understandable reaction.

'We did not do this, I promise. If you come with us, we will tell you all we know,' the man replied. The residents of Merryville all looked at each other skeptical, wondering if they should actually trust these strangers in this even stranger situation. None of them moved straight away, they just sat there like mannequins in a shop window, watching. The man gave them his hand, as did the woman who was standing slightly behind him.

'Who are you?' Jane asked. Sharon seemed to be getting upset on the other side of the room.

'My name is Mark, Mark Noir. This is my colleague Nadia Trott. Now, you must come with us. It is not safe here, they know you are here and will come soon,' Mark said with urgency in his voice and gesturing them to hurry up with his hands.

George stood up and this started a chain reaction and soon they were all up on their feet. All were huddled together and followed Mark and Nadia out of the room and into the bright white corridor. All were nervous and anxious about what kind of world they had entered.

The light seemed to be so bright, no matter where they looked, there was white. They could not escape it, it was as if the light was emanating not just from the ceiling, but from the floor and also from the walls as well. Walking for what felt like hours, travelling from one corridor to another, all of them looking around the same…confused. It was a maze, no one spoke. All that could be heard was the treading feet of them all. Still they carried on walking and did not know where they were going. All of them felt like if something happened, they would not be able to find their way back. Their eyes had all adjusted to the white and they could now look around without pain throbbing in their heads.

A dead end was presented at the end of the corridor and it seemed that they could go no further.

'What now?' George asked. 'Did you take a wrong turn?'

'Nope, this is it,' Mark said. He turned to what seemed like the dead end. There was a noise and then there was a crack in the wall… a door.

Again, they were in a dull room. There was a light switch which was activated by Nadia and then the room had an ambient glow to it. It would have been relaxing in another time. There were many chairs and they all took a seat.

'Well, what now?' Alex asked.

'Well, that's it really. We hide here, so that they don't see us,' Nadia replied.

'Who... What is going on?' Nora spoke sternly, annoyed by their new situation. She, as well as the others, felt like they just seem to be getting into worse situations all the time. They all longed to have their normal, boring lives back.

'The occupants of this ship,' Mark replied. The Petersons, the Jones' and Nora all looked at each other in complete confusion.

'We will tell you everything, but first we need to eat and get refreshed,' Mark said. The room fell silent. They were all handed a dry meal with a splash of water like substance. None were hungry, James played with his food, he felt sick. The silence fell again, Mark and Nadia could be heard chewing on their meal, every time food was swallowed, it echoed within the walls of their new prison.

'What shall we do?' Jane whispered to George.

'I don't know, wait I suppose. Hopefully they will tell us something,' He replied.

'What is that sound?' Sharon asked. They all

listened closely, it sounded like footsteps of someone running. It was, it got louder and louder. Then a knock sounded, the door opened, floods of white light came rushing in and blinded them all once again.

Another man stood before them, he was tall and slim, Long brown hair and hazel eyes.

'Everyone, this is Vincent,' Mark introduced him. 'He's another colleague of ours. There were more of us but the others were taken by those... things.'

'I had to run, they nearly caught me,' Vincent said, grabbing at some of the liquid in the metal cans. Beads of sweat were running down his long face and dripped from his chin, making a splat sound as it hit the floor.

'I'm sorry, but who exactly are these people and what do they want with us?' Jane asked. 'I'm getting tired of your stalling.' The three colleagues stopped what they were doing and looked at each other.

'Ok, I guess we owe you that,' Mark said. 'Now that we are all here, we can begin.'

'Thank you,' Nora said, she thought that now maybe they could come to some conclusion, she wanted life to begin with a fresh start.

The three colleagues put down their plastic tubs and metal drink canisters and moved everything to the side. They cleared a space and pulled up their chairs. Now, huddled together, it reminded James of the classroom discussions he had had in school. He hated those lessons, but would do anything to have them back again. A normal life, a dream that he was not hopeful of becoming true.

'I would say get ready to hear something unbelievable, but I'm sure that you all have an open mind, especially because of what you have just been through. Your devastating journey is about to get a whole lot more complicated,' Mark said. 'I suppose it all started about a year ago…'

Chapter 5

Mark, Nadia and Vincent were all sitting close. Mark sipped at his drink, then looked back at them all. The Merryville residents were all sat on the edge of their seats, all were intrigued about what they were going to reveal.

The silence was thick in the room as Mark was pondering where to begin their story from.

'We started off as a team of five. We were working for a company who was preparing to conduct secret space travel, TechSpace they were called. We all were selected to participate in this venture. We all had emails which had vague details and a link to press if we were interested. At first we thought it might be a virus email, but they were persistent and kept on sending emails. We signed an agreement of confidentiality and then told what we had let ourselves in for. They told us that they wanted to reach further into space than anyone had gone before, all in the name of research. It all sounded exciting and we agreed to continue.' He took another sip of his drink, the liquid could be heard running down his throat. His appearance showed that he was nervous and anxious about telling anyone about it, the thought of reliving it all again seemed to be showing, though he continued.

'We were all trained and pushed to breaking point, they made sure that we were ready one hundred percent. Six months went by, we all gave up our day jobs to become full time researchers. The day we signed up for had arrived, well it was night time, early hours of the morning. The five of us stood in front of a space rocket. It was smaller in comparison to some I have seen. We took our seats and the countdown commenced. We were all nervous and shaking uncontrollably. We did not know what to expect, we have no expertise in these things. We were told to report back with anything we saw and to take pictures and videos using some specialized equipment they could monitor. So we took off.'

'The shuttle sped up, faster and faster. I was scared for all of us. It was frightening. We flew into the night sky and before we knew it we were miles from Earth. When zero gravity hit we saw the Earth standing below us. We were floating through space. It all looked the same, the stars still seemed to be so far away. We lived in space for three weeks, taking pictures, videos and writing logs.'

'After the three weeks, we started to get worried, we were not receiving any information or instruction. All communication seemed to have stopped and we were still in space, not knowing what we needed to do next. Any attempt tried to make communication seemed to fail.'

'We gave up. We thought that that was the end, our food supply was running low and the power supply to our shuttle was getting low.' Mark stopped and couldn't control himself any longer. He looked towards Nadia, signaling her to continue. His head drooped and he sat still staring down towards the floor.

Nadia took Mark's hand and continued where he had left off.

'I remember that night, it was getting colder as the power supply dropped. We tried to maneuver the shuttle to get on some sort of path home using the power we had left. When we turned the shuttle around, we saw something moving towards us in the distance. A small thing in the distance to begin with, but then it got closer and rapidly became bigger. An eye moving towards us. When it was really close it seemed to break apart in the middle and before we knew what was happening, our ship was inside of it. That is where we are now.'

'We were told not to worry and that our safety

would be guaranteed as long as we cooperated. All of us were scared and I'm not ashamed to say that we all cried as well. How could you not, it felt like a horror movie…unreal.'

'We all blacked out for a while, when we woke up we were in the room we found you guys in. It was cold and I can still hear the sound of that haunting dripping pipe in my sleep at night. We were sat in there for a while and then a bright light appeared before us. To say we were scared would be an understatement. It was pure terror. Our eyes could not adjust in time, they dragged our colleagues; Matt and Thomas from the room and shut the door behind them. It all happened so quickly, none of us saw who was there. The sound of Matt and Thomas crying as they were dragged out still rings in my ears when I am alone.' Nadia took a sip of her own drink, a tear escaped her eye and travelled down her face.

'We decided that waiting around for them to come back was maybe not such a great idea, so we looked outside the room we were being held in, luckily it was not locked. Blinded by the white light, but we carried on regardless, it wasn't long before we stumbled across this room and set up base camp. This had been our living quarters ever since. Going out can be risky but it is a task that each of us have to endure. So many times we have nearly been caught by them. We have to go out also for food and water, they have a store room with dried foods and water up above, though it tastes like something you might tread in, it's the only thing we have got to keep us alive.'

Nadia looked towards Mark, who was beginning to get himself under control. She hugged him. Vincent had turned his back to everyone half way through the retelling. The Merryville residents were all listening very closely.

'So how do we get off of this thing?' George asked.

'We do not know, we have looked, believe me,' Nadia explained.

'What are we supposed to do then, just live here with no plan of action?' Jane asked, anger entering her voice.

'We are still trying to find a way, but they have literally thought of everything to keep us here,' Mark said.

'Well, do you at least know what they want from us?' Jane asked. Mark, Nadia and Vincent all remained silent. The answer was obvious, they did not know. All their hearts sank in their chest, Sharon was trying to keep strong, Alex was comforting her as best he could. Nora seemed too in shock to say anything.

'Who are these people?' Nora asked.

'Not who... what. They are not people like us. They are, I don't know how to say this without sounding completely insane. I suppose they are some sort of extra-terrestrial being,' Nadia said.

'Aliens?'

Nadia nodded. 'I suppose they must be, they do not look like us.'

'I've heard enough, this is completely crazy. I am going to wake up in a minute, this is a bad nightmare,' Jane said very angrily now. 'I know this is a dream,' she continued. She knew that it wasn't deep down, but the words seemed to calm her down a little. She held James in her arms and started to sob loudly.

'Now there are more of us, maybe we could try and get to the bottom of this,' George suggested. Nadia, Mark and Vincent all looked at each other again.

'Maybe we could, but first I think we need to sleep on it and come up with a plan of some sort, we do not want to just charge in all guns blazing. They are dangerous, God only knows what they have done with Matt and Thomas.' Nadia said.

'I'm sorry, what exactly are we dealing with here Nadia?' Nora asked, sounding annoyed.

'They call themselves the Ocularits...'

∞

'I see that they have now been moved to a not so secret location. Do they think that they are actually safe? The ignorance of them. Thinking that they can outsmart me. Though I think that I will let them be for the moment. I want to catch them in a trap like a pest. Soon enough they will want to have food, then snap! Ha, I have waited a long time for this, a few more hours won't hurt, though I need this to be completed soon.'

Chapter 6

The night was long for all the new arrivals. Time did not seem to have any meaning. There was no telling what time it was, they all seemed to be lost without a compass in an unending maze. Their heads were soaking up all the new information that they had received. All of them thought about what the next step would be, or could be.

The minutes turned to hours and they all sat in the gloomy room, staring at each other. They were all desperately thinking of something… something to help. James had fallen asleep on Jane's leg and George was pacing the room, the same as he did when he is angry, though anger may not be the correct emotion, maybe fury might be more on the mark. Nora was comforting an upset Sharon and Alex.

'So these Ocularits are not human?' George asked, knowing the answer to his question before he even spoke.

'Definitely not, I feel that they are very

dangerous. Matt and Thomas were the smartest of us all and they have not managed to escape them. I do not even know where they are. This vessel we are in is so huge. Like a labyrinth of long white corridors and dead ends,' Vincent replied.

'How are we just discovering them now? With all the space travel and experiments the planet has done. Surely we would have picked up on something like this?'

'You would have thought so. Maybe someone did know. Maybe that is the reason we got sent out here in the first place. We will never know now, Earth is destroyed, we may never know if anyone has survived.' Reality then hit all of them when the words were calculated in their brains.

George continued to pace the small room, which seemed to be closing in after every stride.

Some time went by without any conversation and everyone was beginning to get hungry and thirsty. Exhaustion was creeping up on them all. Waves of yawning started.

'I'm going to go out and get some food from the store room,' Nadia announced. She stood up and composed herself. Starting for the door, George approached her.

'I will come too.'

'NO,' she almost shouted at him. It set him back a few steps. He was shocked, as she had hardly said anything the whole time. It was apparent to everyone that Mark was the captain of this team and Nadia and Vincent were the crew. 'I mean, it's not safe. I'm taking a big risk, I do not want to be responsible for you also. Your time will come, believe me, but until you get some grip on what is happening, this vessel just isn't safe. You need to get yourself used to the environment up here, you may not notice it just yet, but you will soon,' she continued. Gingerly, Nadia opened up the door to the endless corridors which lead outside of the room and then she was gone.

'Ignore her,' Mark said. 'Nadia is just looking out for you all. She will not even let me or Vincent get the water or food. It has been her job since we arrived and I think sometimes, she becomes a bit overprotective about it.'

George resumed with his pacing, up and down the room. It got quiet once again, it seemed to creep into their bones. Every passing second could be felt, a slight throbbing.

There were no windows or portholes to see outside into space. They were completely isolated and alone. It was hard for all of them to keep track on what was happening.

'Nadia has been gone ages,' Jane said, looking towards the other crew members with worry and concern. 'How long do these trips usually take?'

'Not to worry, Nadia always takes longer, I suppose that's why they have not spotted her before, she is very careful about what she is doing,' one of the crew members replied, Jane was too exhausted to figure out which one actually said it, she supposed it didn't really matter anyway.

More minutes past and they could just about hear something in the distance approaching, Nadia's footsteps. She had made it back safe and had brought some of the water like substance and some dried foods.

'This is all I could manage, they would have seen me if I'd been a second longer,' she explained. No one else spoke, Mark handed out the food and drink and they all ate. It felt so good to the residents of Merryville to eat something, they were not used to this sort of living, rationing and scrounging, the food they had had didn't fill them up. James soon finished off his food and still felt hungry. They all felt it as they finished one by one. Their stomachs felt like they were filled with pure acid, gurgling around deep in their guts.

'I have decided that tomorrow, we will take George and Alex out and try and get them used to the area. I mean, we need you to know, just in case something happens to us. Who knows what's around the corner,' Mark announced. Nadia looked at him in horror.

'I don't think they are ready, they have only been here five minutes,' she said.

'I know, but as there are more of us, we have more chance of being found and if something happens then someone needs to know where to get supplies. I am almost certain they are looking for you all as we speak, they know that you are on board.'

George felt almost a sense of responsibility at this latest announcement, Alex on the other hand felt his heart stop in his chest and the feeling of dread fell upon him. He felt like he could not just leave Sharon, knowing that every time he left the room, might be the last time he saw her. Deep down the dislike for the plan grew, though he did not want to protest, feeling a sense of responsibility the same as George. He did not want to look weak and afraid in front of everyone else.

The two men decided to go with them and then they continued to sip their funny tasting beverages. It felt as if the room was getting darker, their eyes were tired from all the events that have happened. The Petersons and the Jones' fell asleep shortly after and Nora followed suit.

When all was silent, Nadia and Mark turned to each other.

'Are you sure you are making the right decision?' Nadia whispered to Mark.

'We need to show them. That's the end of the discussion.'

'What if the Ocularits get them?'

'We just need to hope and pray that they show them mercy.'

∞

'I have spotted the specimen I want for this project. I will check with my guard to make sure that we have everything in place for this. Though it does sicken me to think that I'm walking the same floor as them, even breathing the same air. I hope tomorrow brings us another step closer to what we have been looking forward to so much. This project will be the making of us all, I can feel in through my body. I can feel that something good is going to happen. Soon enough, I will become the ruler of the Galaxy. The council are so naive, I do not think they even know about Earth being destroyed yet. Apart from the humans being cozy in their hideout, everything else is going to plan.'

Chapter 7

Alex was abruptly awoken in the night, the room had become dark. The lights were off. He could hear Nadia talking, to Mark he presumed. It was deadly silent apart from the echo of her voice. He did not want to move, in case it startled anyone else awake. He just laid there, waiting for the others to stir. How long had he been asleep? What was the time? Was there even any time here? So many questions plagued his mind.

Alex's mind drifted to other things. He thought about home, wondering if any of his family had survived and what they might be doing now in the barren wasteland planet, Earth. The questions rose in his brain again and he could not seem to shift them. He then remembered that himself and George were going out of the safe room, the feeling of nausea bubbled in his stomach at the thought. He desperately tried to think of a way out of the venture.

It's not as if I can say I have a doctor's

appointment. He tried to think of other things. He wasn't really worried about himself, he was worried about Sharon, she could be so weak. He worried that if anything happened to him, she would lose it, breakdown, do something silly. He would not let that happen.

The clock inside his mind ticked by and he failed to hear Nadia's presence. Had she gone to sleep? He was not really paying much attention while his mind was drifting. His thoughts stopped asking him questions, he suddenly became aware that the floor he was on was very uncomfortable and wondered how he even managed to sleep in the first place. The seams in his clothing seemed to protrude into his skin making him restless. He gingerly moved around to find a more comfy spot. Turning, he was just in time to see the door to the room closing. Someone gone out? Looking around the now dark room he failed to see anything. Alex could not even see how many silhouettes there were laying on the floor.

He still tried to find his comfy spot. His mind began to think about more things, before he knew it, he was asleep again. Dreaming. Dreaming of what life was like, before all this happened.

A noise sounded in the room where they were, alerting them all awake. It was only a slight sound, but very high pitched, like a dog whistle for people. It made Nora and James cover their ears. Mark swiftly got up and flicked a nearby switch.

'What was that horrendous noise?' Nora asked.

'Our alarm clock, we wired it up not long after discovering this room. We wanted to try and keep to Earth time as much as we could so our body clocks wouldn't be too messed up. That is the plan anyway, but after the state of Earth I doubt if we will ever return,' Mark explained.

'What time is it set to?'

'Seven in the morning, or there about,' he replied. He looked around at everyone, they all looked tired, still and scared. He thought back to when he and the other crew members came on board this vessel, he remembered feeling the same as they looked.

Breakfast was served, it was a dry powder. James thought that it tasted like baby sick. The others, so hungry, ate it without a second thought. Even Sharon, who had been off her food since everything started happening, ate it without a hesitation.

'Who went out last night?' Alex asked, remembering the door closing when he was struggling to find another position to lay in.

'No one, we do not leave in the night. We only

leave when there is someone else awake,' Mark replied. He looked towards Nadia and Vincent, both were finishing their meals and did not seem to hear what was being said.

'But I thought I saw the door open last night,' he was not satisfied with the answer, he was sure of what he had seen.

'I can assure you that we were all here, I am a very light sleeper and I would know. Trust me, maybe it was your eyes playing tricks on you. They do that to you sometimes in here, it seems like sometimes the walls are closing in. Sometimes you see things in the corner of your eyes. It's all in your mind, Alex,' Mark insisted. Alex let it go, he could see that Mark was becoming annoyed at his questioning.

The last of the breakfast was devoured and Mark tidied the room slightly, to make more space. He produced a large leaf of paper and on it was a map of the vessel they were on, the residents of Merryville assumed. They all looked upon it with complete concentration and never looking away.

'Here we are,' Mark pointed to a room off one of the numerous corridors. 'The food supply is here,' he pointed to a room called The Chamber. It was a hexagon shaped room with only one entrance. 'You will take the route here to reach it,' he ran his finger from the room they were in to The Chamber which included; one long corridor, two short ones and a short cut through two small rooms.

'Where are these things we need to watch out for?' George asked.

'They reside in the Optical room most of the time, but they have guards walking around in all places of the vessel. We will just need to move slowly and carefully and if we see any of them and will just have to wait until they are gone,' he explained. Alex looked towards Sharon who was looking more worried than ever, tears began threatening in her eyes. He took her hand and pulled her close.

'It will be fine,' he reassured her, though he was not sure really. He had no idea what might happen. He was terrified now that the time had come.

George was hugging James and Jane and Nora dabbled between both families.

'Are you two ready?' Nadia asked. George and Alex both nodded, neither of them wanted to speak.

'Follow me and you should be fine. Let's go.'

Chapter 8

Alex could feel a bead of sweat run down the side of his face, not because he was hot, he was scared. Alex, George and Nadia walked in a conga line down the first long corridor. It was bright with a white shine, at first it was hard to focus on anything, then after a few seconds exposed to the bright light it did not feel so bad. It was quiet, so quiet that the smallest noise would seem loud. Everything looked the same, the walls, floor and ceiling all seemed so clean.

Reaching the end of the first corridor there was a door to the left. Nadia pushed it forward and it moved silently on its fixture. They entered the room, it was dark, cold and gloomy. The space was a complete contradiction to the corridor they had just left. Again, taking a few seconds for their eyes to adjust, they continued through the room, maneuvering around obstacles in their path. Nadia stopped and turned towards the two men, they could just about make out her serious face, staring at them.

'Right, when we get out of this door, we need to move much faster. This next corridor leads us right past the Optical room, where *they* normally are. You will notice it as it has a green light emanating off it. Once past this room take the next room on the right, got it?' She said. George and Alex both looked at each other and then both nodded in sync. She opened the door letting in the bright light once again, she counted to three under her breath and went. They all moved quickly and quietly down the short corridor. Alex saw the Optical room before anyone else, the lime green light around it, made it look sinister. The room came and went, before they knew it they were again in complete darkness as they entered the second room. This room like the first was dull and depressing. There was a little light shining from an unknown source, they did not stay long enough to look.

'Right, this is it. We have one small corridor left and the room at the end is the one with the supply in. Be ready for anything, they sometimes reside in The Chamber. When we enter the room turn immediately left and duck behind the mental canisters there.

They were off again, they walked the small corridor more quickly than Alex wanted. George had also began to show signs of nerves, he was shaking slightly and his brow was wet.

'This is it,' Nadia said when they reached the end of the corridor. 'Anything could be behind this door so be quick,' she added. '3…2…1…'

'How long do these trips usually take?' Sharon asked, scared for her husband. She knew full well that he did not want to go in the first place, but he didn't want to look like a wimp.

'You cannot really put a time on it, it depends whether the Ocularits are about,' Mark replied.

'It will be ok,' Nora said, comforting Sharon. Jane looked upon the situation with skepticism, whilst supporting James' head whilst he slept. The room fell silent, no one could think of anything to say to lighten the mood. All were scared for them, out there, where they could be hurt… or worse killed.

'There is no need to worry girls, Nadia is a fine woman and will keep them both safe. She has done this trip more than us and knows the route like the back of her hand,' Vincent assured them. Sharon did not look assured, she looked like she could faint at any moment. So they waited and did all they could not to think of the situation.

Nadia, George and Alex crept into The

Chamber and did what was instructed of them and went behind the canisters. With their backs pressed against the grey metal, they could feel how cold they were.

'I'll show you where it is from here, you both stay and watch what I do,' Nadia whispered so quietly, it sounded like the wind. The two men watched Nadia with a close eye, waiting to see what she did, memorizing her every move just in case they had to make this trip one day. She went to one door and slid in and then a few minutes later she reappeared with the dried foods. She crept back to where the men were and then she signaled to go. They retraced their steps back out of the empty room, back down the small corridor into the other room at the end. They stood still and caught their breath, adrenaline was rushing through all their bodies.

'Got it, you know what to do now?' She asked them. They both nodded and then they were off again. Nadia first, then George and finally Alex, reassembled in their conga line formation. They crept quickly but silently down the corridor past the Optical room, the green light still threatening them as they went by, suspense hung in the air, reminding them that at any time they could get caught. George was sure that he would dream about this place that night. The threesome walked through the second room without stopping and did the final corridor in one swoop. George recognised the door where they were, his wife and son. Even though he had only been gone a short while, he missed them terribly. At some points George thought that he was never going to see them again and had to quickly come to terms with it. A breath escape him when Nadia opened the door and he could see all their faces looking at them.

Nadia walked in first, followed by George. The door closed behind them and their heart sank in their chest.

'Where's Alex?' Sharon asked.

'I... I don't know he was behind me a second ago,' George replied. Tears rolled down Sharon's eyes immediately. There was a haunted atmosphere in the room.

'Don't panic just yet, he might have just fallen behind,' Nora said. But everyone knew, including Nora and Sharon, what had happened.

No one knew what to say.

Nadia walked back out of the room, maybe to retrace their steps. The air fell cold over all of them, like a blanket of snow. The smell of metal was strong in the air. Sharon tried to keep herself together, at least until Nadia came back.

All they could do was wait...

∞

'Now that we have this specimen, we can proceed with the project. Oh it makes me feel excited to think that everything I have worked towards is all paying off. Although this specimen is the weakest of the group, I admire their courage and bravery for even venturing out. They must not know how I always get my way. Well. They will know soon enough. Bring me the prisoner, let's get this show started. It's going to be a bloodbath let me assure you, ha.'

Chapter 9

The room was gloomy and the air was cold. It felt like the inside of a fridge. The light that was there illuminated his breath, like a puff of smoke escaping from his mouth. It was deadly quiet, except for a humming noise going off somewhere in the distance. He felt alone and scared. Though it was cold, his brow produced small beads of sweat which ran down his face and in his eyes, stinging them profusely.

Trying to move, he quickly found that he had been tied to a chair of some description, similar to the chair in the first room they woke up in, in this unforgiving place. The calls for help were useless, the words kept getting stuck in his throat. His mouth was so dry, he craved a cool glass of water, the thought of it made his mouth even dryer. With eyes becoming more focused on his surroundings, he looked all around and what was there… depressing, grey walls, maybe steel or some other metal, similar to that in the corridor. In one corner there was a table of some description but he could not see what was laying upon it from his angle. Still, he tried to untie himself with no success, the more he tried the more the rope seemed to tighten.

Now and again he thought he saw the shadows on the wall dance in front of his eyes. His mind playing tricks on him, eyes messing with his mind, thoughts of seeing someone in the corner of the room scared him. No one there. He thought about how long he had been here. Black shadowed his vision and he blacked out for a while.

A new sound could be heard coming from afar it seemed. Then a bit louder. It was footsteps. *Was someone coming to help?* He hoped so.

Shadows produced themselves on the other side of the door, they could be seen at the bottom gap leading out of the room. Someone was coming into the dark space, his heart felt like it could have stopped. Fear rose up in him. He held his breath involuntarily it seemed, he had to remind himself to keep breathing. *How can someone forget to breath?* He thought to himself. Then the sound of a lock opening was heard and then the brilliant white light that haunts this place invaded him.

George held Jane and James in his arms, he was scared for their safety, now more than before. Nadia had been gone a while and everyone was on edge, no one said anything. Nora was still trying to comfort Sharon, while Mark and Vincent were looking at the map.

'What is taking them so long?' Sharon almost screamed the words, everyone was taken back. She then embraced Nora again.

'I'm sure they will be here at any moment. Do not worry, Nadia will make sure she gets the job done,' Mark assured her. He looked towards Vincent, signaling him to say something. Unknowing what to say he just agreed with Mark. The two men then conversed a little and then Vincent walked out the room.

'Vincent is just going to go down the corridor a little to see if there is any trace of them,' Mark announced. The door closed on Vincent and then it went quiet once again.

A figure entered the room and shut the door behind itself. He could not work out who or what it was.

'Hello?' He called. 'Who's there?' he asked. There was no reply. He knew there was someone very close, he could hear the clanking of metal and the movement of fabric. 'Talk to me,' he said again.

'Hello,' the voice replied unnervingly.

'Who are you?' He asked.

'My name is Blistrix, the son of the high

emperor. What is your name?' The voice asked.

'A... Alex.'

'Hello Alex, I trust you are having a good time on board our vessel,' the voice said sounding sinister. It carried through the air like a haunting wind.

'What do you want?' Alex called, scared. He thought that he could just breakdown.

'All in good time, but first we have a small problem. You entered The Chamber unauthorized. That room is for Ocularits only,' he said, sounding angrier by the second.

'I, I didn't know.'

'Well, now you do and you need to be punished for this behavior. Listen here you second grade animal. This is a ship run by us, I hate humans. Humans are vermin, they must be caught and must be destroyed. WE WILL RULE,' he shouted across the room at him. Alex did not reply to this. He just sat where he was and did not move a muscle.

A few seconds passed. The sound of rustling ceased a little, then a click started a light just above his head. He could only see a few steps ahead of him, the rest of the room was in shadow.

'Show yourself,' Alex demanded. There was silence and then Blistrix walking into the beam of light. What was presented to Alex was the stuff of nightmares. He felt like he could have fainted but he denied himself to do so. He analyzed the being with interest and fear in equal measures.

Blistrix was wearing a full purple and blue robe which dragged a little on the metal floor behind him. His arms were long and his fingers went to a point, they looked sharp. Alex thought about how much damage could be caused by them. His collar was high. His head was what shocked him the most. Unlike the aliens he saw on TV and in movies, these never had a face. Instead of a head they just had a big eyeball on top of their neck. The iris and pupil darting around everywhere, searching and watching.

'Now, do you like what you see, filth?' It asked. Alex shook his head.

'How are you talking, you have no mouth?' Alex was curious.

'All the Ocularits are set up with a device that sounds out our thoughts into all the languages, in all the universes.' Blistrix explained.

'Why do you want to hurt us... humans? Why did you burn our planet?'

'Revenge. Earths pollution caused our planet to burn. Sure it might not have been much but our atmosphere was so fragile that it burned quickly. You all must pay for the lives that have been lost.'

Just then the door opened again and someone or something else walked into the room.

'Now we can begin the procedure,' Blistrix said. Alex looked puzzled and petrified. 'Pass me the tool,' Blistrix instructed the new arrival. Alex could not figure out what this one looked like, but he assumed they all looked the same. He brought this tool into the light and it looked rusty, old and dirty. Alex could not find the energy inside him to scream for help, there was nothing else he could do.

'Don't worry,' Blistrix said. 'It will only hurt until you die.' Then he started the machine, which sounded like a dentist drill. He watched this thing come towards him, spinning fast. It was so loud, the sound deafened him and all he could hear was a constant buzz, then a pain went through his whole body, then there was nothing, but not before he saw his insides start to splatter around the room, like something from a horror movie.

∞

'Well, that was fun. I haven't felt a rush like that since the crew came aboard. I feel excited deep down in the pit of my stomach. This is the meaning of the word joy, I'm sure of it. The council still has no idea what is going on. I'm so thrilled. Ha, soon I'll be the ruler of this race and the humans will be gone. Nothing makes me happier. Well this is not time to stand around feeling marvelous, we have

two more sacrifices left to make, let's make them good ones. I know exactly which ones to choose.'

Chapter 10

There was a faint sound of footsteps approaching the 'safe room' and all who were present were watching with anticipation. The sound echoed off the long corridor walls, it sounded like something from a nightmare. The bright light from beyond the walls of the room, pierced their eyes as it struck them again, though they were beginning to get used to it.

'Nadia. Where have you been?' Mark said, breathing a sigh of relief.

'Looking for Alex,' she replied, she seemed out of breath. Her face was wet like she had been crying. Mark did not want to ask, he knew that she would say something, if there was something bothering her.

Nadia looked vacantly around the room. 'Where has Vincent disappeared too?'

'He went looking for you,' Nora replied from the darkest corner of the room. She was still holding Sharon close to her heart as her fragile body slept like a baby in the old woman's arms. It was reminiscent of the Madonna and Child painting they all knew so well, now, like everything else it was just a pile of ashes on earth's surface.

'I didn't see him. I retraced our footsteps,' she said looking towards the others. 'I heard something coming from a room down one of the corridors. I'm not sure what or who it was, so I came back here as soon as I heard it,' she added.

Some time went by and there was no sign of Vincent. It wasn't until thirty minutes or so later that he walked into the room, red faced and out of breath, almost panting, like someone who had just ran a marathon without training. He did not have the energy to even talk, walking to the nearest wall, he turned his back and slid down to the floor. When he caught his breath, he still did not say anything. He looked a bit upset about something, looked depressed and was not like his usual self at all. They knew that he was a quiet person, but he was too quiet.

Everyone was still on edge about whether he would actually say anything at all. He remained in silence. Jane finally asked the question.

'Did you see anything?'

'No,' he replied flatly to her. Jane was taken back at his tone. George looked towards her and did not know what to say. He thought that maybe he should defend his wife in the situation but he did not know what to do.

Nadia walked over to him.

'What is wrong with you?' She asked with soft spoken words, almost a whisper.

'I'm fine,' he replied, again flatly.

'You are being strange. What is wrong? Please tell us.' He did not reply to this and just closed his eyes. Nadia and Mark locked eyes for a second, she shrugged and rejoined the others.

Some time went by and Sharon stirred in Nora's lap. She opened her eyes and looked around, hoping to see her Alex sitting there. He was not.

'Did they find him?' She asked Nadia. Nadia looked at her with sad eyes and simply shock her head slowly from one side to the other. A lone tear rolled down Sharon's face and dripped onto the floor, it echoed through the room. It sounded so far away, just as Sharon now felt so far away from everything without Alex by her side.

'What now then?' She asked. Her eyes looking worried, like that of a lost puppy. No one said anything at first. She saw that Nadia and Mark were in a conversation about something.

'Sharon,' Mark finally said. 'We need to wait for a while. We will find him, but we need to rest for now and then we will go out searching again tomorrow. If those things have him....' he added, then broke off. Sharon could see what else he was going to say in his eyes.

'You mean he might be dead?' She asked. There was silence in the room. The silence was loud and awkward in the cold space. No one knew what to say, though they had been neighbours on Earth for years, they didn't know how to console her.

So they just sat and waited for something unknown.

Chapter 11

Everyone was lost in sleep except for Sharon, who was wide awake and worried about Alex. She was beginning to come to terms with the fact that she may not see him ever again. Quietly sobbing as her eyes focused on the dark and depressing wall, within these walls was her home. She thought that the colour of the surroundings was the definition of depression. She could not think of another time where she felt alone, Alex had always been by her side all her adult life. They had been together when they had to make the extremely difficult decision to put their parents in nursing homes. He was there when they had problems at work. They were together when the thing came down to Earth and put all other minor things into perspective, little niggling feelings were pushed aside the day IT arrived. They had managed to live through all that and now they are somewhere deep in the darkest space and he was no longer with her.

Her mind was replaying Alex's facial

expression in her head, the one he made when they left the room to explore. She could see that he was so scared and would have done anything not to go, but then he wanted to be able to show them all that he had it in him. Her brain kept thinking, bringing her pictures to look at, whilst the tears rolled down her face. She had accumulated a pool of tears on the floor next to her and did not think she could cry much longer. Feeling dehydrated from crying so much, she tried desperately to think about something else. The sandman must be in space somewhere, she was beginning to fall asleep, Sharon was getting worried that he had forgotten about her. Slowly she drifted into the darkness. She did not know if she was travelling to somewhere happy or another terrible nightmare, an event much more frequent.

'Alex, what is that thing?' She asked. Alex was standing beside her holding her hand. He turned, but did not say anything. He just shrugged. 'Oh Alex. Are we going to be ok?'

'I have no idea,' he spoke with muffled words, just barely audible. It was like he was speaking through a wall, the sound muffled and distant.

Her mind drifted further…

'What should we do Father?' Sharon asked, looking around the dark and damp church, the old style candle chandeliers swinging from the rafters above.

'We need to pray for everything and everyone. There is nothing else we can do. God will help and protect us, He will guide us through this disaster. I'm sure of it,' Father Michael reassured her.

'We can't do that. Have you seen what it is doing to the outside world?' Alex asked.

'Indeed I have. I'm sorry there is nothing else I can suggest,' the Father said.

Her mind drifted...

'What have you seen?' Sharon asked.

'I'm not sure. I can't describe it. Quick, grab me the notepad and pen, I'll draw it down,' He asked.

Drifting further...

'We have news on... that thing,' she said to Jane pointing up to the evil looking down on them.

Further...

The Jones' and the Petersons were sitting around a table. Alex brought out a piece of paper.

'An eye,' James said from behind her.

Darkness.

A noise.

Sharon opened up her eyes and heard movement coming from behind her. She wanted to look but something deep down told her not to.

Though her mind wanted to see who it was, maybe someone would be able to make her feel better, though she didn't think they could.

Her body started turning, as if she wasn't doing it. She could see something moving, someone moving. The room was too dark to see who it was. No one else was restless, they were all asleep... or dead she thought, then she heard them breathing.

The movement ceased and then she could see a shadow moving towards the door to the room. As the door opened the white light from the corridor flashed in to reveal Vincent standing there, exiting the room.

Then there was a blanket of darkness again. The room seemed to become much cooler.

What is he up too? She thought. She was extremely tired and her eyes kept drifting off, she struggled to stay away. The desire to sleep was overpowering, the more her body struggled the harder it was to keep her eyes open.

∞

'At first I thought that the thrill of the chase would be fun. This waiting though, it is starting to drive me insane. We need to work much quicker so that we can reach my deadline. I want this whole thing completed as soon as possible. We need to

find a way to lure them out of their so called "safe house". I could just walk right in there and take what I need, but I have come this far undiscovered, I do not intend to fail at the last hurdle. This process is so close to being final, I can see the light at the end of the tunnel.'

Chapter 12

'Sharon... Sharon... Wake up,' a voice called, disturbing her already restless sleep. Her eyes opened and slowly they adjusted slightly. 'You need to eat something, it's been ages. Vincent has just got some more supplies for us all,' it was Jane, she handed Sharon, what she guessed was a green vegetable. Slowly beginning to eat at it, she became hungrier. The more she ate the more her appetite was being restored and looking down at the plate Sharon was surprised when she had finished.

Her eyes gazed around the room and looked over towards Vincent, who was eating a similar dish. Her mind wondered back to the night before, she had seen him go out of the room. Her mind wondered if she should ask, then her mind drifted onto Alex. She felt a fresh feeling of sadness when she again realised that he was not anywhere to be seen. She laid back down on the cold floor and turned towards the wall, just in time as one lone tear fell from her eye, quietly patting the floor.

'We need to go back out there today, to try and find something to help us get off this ship,' George said, noticing that Sharon has detached from the group.

'I admire your optimism, but we have been on here the best part of a year and there is no way,' Nadia replied.

'There are more of us now, can we not confront those... those things. We could maybe find out what they want.'

A laugh escaped Nadia and Mark.

'Seriously guys, I don't think that they are reasonable beings. They have taken two of our crew and also your Alex,' Mark reminded them.

'Have you ever actually tried to communicate with them, they obviously know that we are on the ship somewhere don't they. I think we should try and communicate somehow,' George said, feeling a little annoyed still at their laughter.

'We have never tried. After we came on board and they took Matt and Thomas, they did not look the talkative types,' Nadia said.

'Do they not talk?' Jane asked. Vincent joined the group.

'They do. They communicate through a voice transmitter. They can talk any language in the universe. They do not have mouths you see. They have an eyeball instead of a head and they have long tentacle protrusions instead of fingers. The eye though, it is haunting. The lack of an eyelid makes them stare, always,' Vincent said.

'Hold on, hold on. This is becoming stupid. Why do they not have eyelids? It is so bright out there. None of this makes sense,' Jane was trying hard to get her head around it, she had a pain in her brain trying to make sense of it all.

'Well, like we have said, they are not like us. Sure we have eyelids for all kinds of reasons, we don't know anything else I suppose. Their race have evolved so much more than Humans. The lack of eyelids do not bother them. I think we are forgetting one major thing, they are *not* humans. Who knows how their bodies work,' Vincent was trying to explain the best way he could, he could see on all their faces that the information was just too complicated for them to process.

'How do they hear then? Also where does all this food come from?' Nora asked, changing the subject from eyes to ears.

'They eat through their chest. Their ribcage opens and they insert the food through a pouch. The food, is teleported from earth. They stock up when there is a full moon. The brightness off of the full moon disguises the vessel which lingers behind. They teleport down and get what they need until the next cycle begins,' He answered.

'How do you know all this?' James asked. They all looked towards Vincent with interest. Vincent did not move for a moment or two. He seemed to be thinking about something. He almost seemed to have not heard what James had said at all.

'Because I was captured for a few days. I had loads of time to ask questions. It happened only a couple of days after we came on board, I was on a food run and ran into trouble. It was the head of the Ocularits army that held me hostage. He asked me questions of Earth and what our crew was doing in space. I was introduced to so many of the creatures. I remember sleeping most of the time, I think they drugged me because I cannot remember everything really, some parts are a blank,' Vincent explained.

The residents of Merryville just stared at him with complete attention, even after he had finished. No one else said anything. Vincent replayed what he could of those days in his mind.

'I...I'm sorry,' Jane said, she genuinely was.

'That's ok. The point I'm getting at is that these things can't be reasoned with,' he reiterated.

There was a cold atmosphere in the room and it felt slightly damp. The longer they all sat there, the longer they had to find faults with everything. Their minds thought about days which have past, happier days. The memories that were deep in their brain, some were stubborn and did not want to be relived. They all thought to themselves whether they would ever have any more happy memories.

∞

'We need to reevaluate the timescales of this project. I have a feeling that the Ocularits council know something. They have been acting very strange, hiding things and silencing as I walk into a room. Even my father, Izazon, has been acting suspicious. We will not do anything out of the ordinary for a few days. We need to be duties as usual. This means nothing to draw attention to ourselves. We need to throw them off the scent a little, or it will be only a matter of time before they all come investigating. We are so close, it is frustrating that we now need to wait. Go about your jobs and soon we will come together to continue.'

Chapter 13

A few days past by and not much else happened, they all continued to live in fear and isolation. All the survivors grew further and further apart. The residents of Merryville hardly knew each other anymore. Their brains were all in auto pilot mode, from the time they opened their eyes to the time they slept again. Monotonous days on end, doing nothing. Jane and George hardly spoke, they had nothing else to talk about. James was the only one who could at least try to string a conversation along. Sharon spent most of her time sleeping, she had had darker thoughts about giving herself up to the Ocularits and being with Alex, though she wasn't sure that he was dead, she just assumed. Nora spent her time trying to support the others. She seemed, to everyone else, to be unmoved by everything that had happened. The crew spent time going to get food and other supplies for the group.

'I don't want to be here anymore,' Sharon said.

Her body did not move as she said this. It seemed like she was telling herself this information rather than anyone else. No one reacted to this comment, though Nora did comfort her a little.

'I know hunny, we just need to be strong for each other,' Nora said. Sharon sighed and then closed her eyes and nodded off almost instantly.

'This is ridiculous,' Jane said. 'We have been up here for over a week,' she thought a little. 'Has it been a week? I have no idea, time is so strange here. We need to do something, we cannot just sit around until we die. Anyway where are they going to get the food from now that they have destroyed Earth, surely there is only a limited supply,' she continued.

'I agree,' Mark said. 'We need to figure out a plan. As for the food, I have no idea. The food supply is still being added too, so they must be getting it from somewhere. Maybe it is something we could ask. But only if they are willing to cooperate.'

Everyone sat in a state of shock that he was actually going to try and help the situation. Jane felt a little glimmer of hope deep down in her stomach.

'What do you suggest we do?' George asked.

'Well I have been thinking about what you said the other day… you know, about confronting them. I think we should try. I mean, we have nothing left to lose,' Mark replied. Nadia darted her eyes at this revelation.

'It's too dangerous,' Nadia said.

'I think it will be ok. I have faith,' Mark struck back. There was a sound coming from Sharon, a laugh.

'Father Michael had faith. Where is he now?' Sharon said without looking at anyone. It sounded to the others that the sound was coming more from the walls rather than from a human, her voice droned through the floor making it vibrate slightly. There was silence from the other residents of Merryville, as they thought about the Father and how he had tried to help each of them. They all wondered what had actually happened to him in those final days on Earth. Did he sacrifice himself?

The day carried on and they all thought about the best plan of action in confronting these strange creatures. James had the most ideas, being a space and science enthusiast the others listened with interest.

The hours went by and the plans seemed to be pulling together. There were moments when they all drifted away from the idea, thinking it was silly. How could the Eye creatures be compassionate and reasonable to their questions and requests? They had all the questions planned out, they knew what needed to be asked. The planning came to an end and then a Mexican wave of yawns started.

'First thing tomorrow, we will go to The Chamber. We will walk in with our heads held high and we will demand to see the one in charge,' Mark said. Then the conversation went onto other topics. They had worked hard with the plan all day and now were all tired and needed to rest. They had a feeling that the next day would be busy. It was not long until everyone was bedded down for sleep.

Nora awoke to the sound of rustling. She gingerly lifted up her head to see if there was anyone moving around and could not see anyone... not at first. Then, a dark figure standing on the other side of the room emerged, she slowly picked up her glasses and positioned them on the end of her nose. She still could not make out who it was. It was quiet and she was aware that her breathing was becoming louder with every breath taken. The shadow moved towards the door, still blacked in mystery. The door opened and the brilliant white from the corridor flooded into the room momentarily. She did not manage to see who it was, visible was only a fuzzy figure walking out of the room. By the time her eyes were focused again, the door had closed.

She looked at all the others, trying to find out who had left the room. She could not see over the other side of the room. Nora did not want to move, in case of waking the others, she knew that it was going to be a struggle getting through the next day.

Nora closed her eyes and tried to sleep once again.

∞

'Well, they are finally leaving that hiding place. I could not be happier, finally I will have the pieces to complete my project. With them leaving, we must take this opportunity to take the sacrifices needed. Hopefully the council are still too blind to see what is happening. The council will blame Izazon for everything and then I'll be the ruler of this race. We will take over planets and universes, the plans are endless. I have such high hopes for the future. No time to stand and wait, we need to prepare the equipment. The revival is close at hand.'

Chapter 14

Restless dreams plagued them all. They all tossed and turned, uncomfortable. Each one of them worried, nervous and nauseous about what might happen. As their energy rose, so did their fears and anxieties. George was the first to sit up and admit that he wasn't going to be able to sleep anymore.

His eyes scanned around the room at all the worried bodies laid out before him. *How did we get here?* He thought to himself. The cogs in his mind, desperately trying to find an answer. Jane was next to him, staring up at the ceiling and James was in the same trance-like state. They all had their own thoughts about what is going to become of them. George could feel his eyes were heavy, as if he hadn't managed to get any sleep at all. He was suddenly overcome with a desire to sob, sob his heart out and just give up, barely managing, George held it in. *Stay strong. Hopefully it will all be over soon,* he hoped.

Sharon was the next one to admit defeat from

sleep. She looked over at George and felt saddened by the way he looked. It was clear that he was deep in thought and so didn't say anything to break it. Further thoughts of Alex came into her head and played out like a silent movie, simple pictures, reminding her of good times that have long since past and present nightmares. *Will I see you again? Maybe today?*

The whole room had a thick atmosphere. It was as if the room was physically filling up with their thoughts. Jane closed her eyes once again for one final attempt at some sleep... nothing. She felt silly just lying there with her eyes closed. It was clear to her that it wasn't going to happen and held George's arm for some comfort.

Nora felt as if her eyes were carrying suitcases under them. She was so tired, but could not sleep. She was apprehensive about what might happen, as they all were. She thought back to her last few days on Earth, she had been so confused, wandering from one place to another. She was tired a lot then as well, she thought that maybe her body was just used to it now.

'Are we ready?' Mark asked them all. He looked out at all the scared looking faces, thinking that maybe this was too ambitious and too soon. *Too late now,* he thought. Mark went out of the room first, then they all followed in a conga line; Mark, George, Jane, James, Nora, Sharon, Vincent and Nadia. They all had the appearance of military, the way that their steps were in sync. No one said anything. They walked down the first corridor and then walked into a room. It occurred to George that it was the same route they had taken before.

'Are we all here?' Mark asked. Everyone replied. The room in which they now reside was dark and smelled like rust and blood. The smell caught them all in the back of the throat. It was not long before Mark carried on through the next corridor, it looked miles long this time.

The green light from the Optical room buzzed as they passed by. There were no guards outside, relief showed on all their faces at that. So they carried on and soon reached the second dark and smelly room.

'Everyone OK?' Mark asked.

'Um... Mark, Nadia and Vincent are not here. There is no one behind me,' Sharon explained. Everyone felt their heart sink deep in their chest. They all remained completely silent for a moment. All that could be heard was the sound of everyone breathing rapidly in fear and confusion.

'What do you mean?' He asked feeling silly after he said it, they are no longer in the line. 'Did you not hear anything?'

'No, they were quiet,' she replied. 'What shall we do?' She asked.

'We can't turn back now, we need to carry on and face these monsters,' he insisted. They carried on through the dull, gloomy room and then the white light from the final corridor hit them all as they walked out.

'Well, Well. I've been waiting for you. I'll be sure this time you do not get away quite so easily,' Blistrix said to Vincent, who was looking around at the depressing room he was in.

'You monster. What are you doing?' He shouted at him. Anger and fear rose up in his body. Feeling restricted his eyes looked down to his arms. As he looked down, in the dull light he could just make out the cuffs which were holding him in place. His eyes did not seem to want to focus, it was like he had been drugged by something. He was not sure.

'All will become clear Vincent. Well, maybe not for you, I'm going to kill you. Rest assured, you will not be killed in vain. We need only two more vile humans to complete the sequence.'

'What sequence. What are you talking about?'

'Silence,' he yelled at Vincent. He closed the gap between them and his eye was centimeters away from Vincent. Just one huge, haunting eye, staring him out. Recoiling back a little, Vincent could hear some clanging of some description. 'Pass me the gag,' he called to his assistant. Before Vincent could find any words he was restricted of speech.

'That's better. I can think straight now. We have been waiting for you to come out of hiding, though we knew where you were anyway. I thought it was more fun waiting, so I could catch you like the irritating rat that you are. Everything about you screams disease and destruction... humans are all the same.' Vincent tried to speak but just could not get the words to sound through the gag.

There was a deadly silence for a while. Then Blistrix came into view again, equipped with a rusty, sharp implement. Vincent could not scream, he was frozen with so much fear.

'Now, you disgusting little pig... brace yourself.' He chuckled to himself as he got closer and the instrument that he was holding began to spin. It span faster and faster. It was inches away from his face, then centimeters then there was red. He had enough time to feel the deep pain that was being caused. He saw his own blood being splattered around the room. Red faded to black.

'Only one more little fly to go and then we will have enough for the revival.'

Chapter 15

Her heart was thumping in her chest as the door to The Chamber came into clear view. She had to breathe in deeply to ease her anxiety levels. All her thoughts could do was think of the worst, what could be behind the door and what might happen to them. Jane looked towards George with worry, he held her hand. James was already holding his mother's hand since Vincent and Nadia disappeared.

She continued to look ahead at the door, it was too close now. It was uncomfortably close, the corridor was not that long to begin with. They approached it at a quick speed.

Sharon looked behind herself and could not see anything there, though she had a feeling that she was being watched. Nora could see that she was beginning to become a shadow of her former self. Sharon smiled slightly at Nora, she replied with a small smile herself. She felt like she had nothing else to lose, she had lost her home, her husband and was on the edge of insanity.

'Right. On three we will enter,' Mark said. He looked around at everyone and they all nodded in agreement and understanding.

'One…'

Sharon could feel her heart begin to thud deep within her chest. She could almost hear nothing but the beating.

'…two…'

Nora noticed that her hands were clammy. Though she did not feel that nervous, she was worried about the unknown. The Petersons were holding hands, united as one.

'…three…'

Nadia watched as Blistrix dismembered her fellow crew member. They had been through so much together, she knew that this would happen, but she could not bring herself to come to terms with it. Her mind drifted to the moment she first met Blistrix.

They had been on board the vessel for only a few hours. Blistrix kidnapped her whilst Vincent and Mark had been asleep. The feeling of certain doom covered her whole body, she was wrapped in the knowledge that she could well be dead in a few minutes. Nadia remembered those feelings vividly. But he spared her life. He needed her help to capture the others, in return he promised not to cause harm to her. He also promised that after the ordeal was over, she would inherit the Ocularits people and rule alongside Blistrix. It was a promise she hoped that he wouldn't keep, she knew that if she was the only human, she would feel so alone. Nadia really did not want to take Blistrix up on his offer, but the coward in her did not want to die. There was a sound of clanging metal and she was brought back to the here and now. The here and now where she had to be convincingly cold hearted.

'That's that then,' Blistrix said to Nadia. 'Though humans are the scum of the universe, you have shown great ability. Thank you for your service. Thank you for your dedication,' he continued.

'No problem. I didn't like him that much anyway. Shame it wasn't that Mark though, he really rubs me up the wrong way. Even Sharon would have been a blessing, all she does is cry about that loser Alex.'

'Ha, well you never know what is waiting. I might just kill them all in the end anyway, just for my enjoyment. Its infuriating watching them walk around my ship. Stealing my food.' Nadia just listened. Fascinated by her partner in crime.

'What are we going to do about your superior? The high emperor,' she asked.

'Don't worry my dear. He's old. He is losing his mind. I will just explain to the Ocularits Council that he knowingly pulled a lever that torched the Earth to ashes. They will never even know that it was me that wanted the humans gone forever. I really do hate them. With their mocking little eyes.'

'That plan is brilliant. They will never suspect.'

'You do not need to tell me that. I know I'm brilliant, that is why I will be much better in charge here. The army is completely on my side. With the revival just around the corner as well. We are at the beginning of a new era. It is exciting. Ocularits will soon be populating the universe.'

'What is this revival anyway? Why is it so important?' Nadia asked, curious about what she had been working towards. Blistrix lone eye looked up to her, the veins in the whites were pumping with blood.

'All in good time. All in good time. It will be revealed sooner than you think.'

He walked towards the door and turned and looked towards Nadia one last time before leaving the room. Nadia was then left, left with the destruction that she caused. Blood flooded the room, thick and velvet red. Vincent was unrecognizable.

'Well, there you go. That's the price you pay when you get caught,' she said to the mutilated corpse. She laughed a little with guilt. 'You made my life much easier. I have noticed that you have been a different man since the others arrived. Quieter and I would say mysterious. It was easy to move around whilst you were acting so suspiciously, they never had a clue, especially with your sleepwalking.'

She looked around the grey, cold room, then refocused back on Vincent.

'I guess the others will know soon. They will have a shock,' she said. She stood up as a tear was forming in the corner of her eye.

'Nice knowing ya,' the room now only occupied the late Vincent Wolfe.

Chapter 16

The door to The Chamber opened, revealing the minimalistic room beyond, they all walked into the wide space. It was cold, but well lit. The grey metal walls were common here. Everywhere they looked it was the same depressing shade. There were a variety of creates around and looked more like a store room than anything else. It was silent, the door slammed behind them. Within all their bodies, they could feel the beating of their hearts.

'Oh, how nice of you to join us,' a voice said. There were a few Ocularits standing before them, but without any mouths it was difficult to decide which one was talking. They all wore similar attire, two were in purple gowns and the other was wearing a green gown with a rather large headdress type accessory.

'Is that what you would call it....*nice*?' Mark asked.

'Who are you?' Sharon shouted from behind the group, feeling more confident with numbers.

'Well. My name is Izazon, I am the high emperor, I run this colony. I did wonder when you would venture out. I hope the journey here wasn't too traumatizing,' he said to them.

'Why did you destroy our world?' Jane asked.

'Destroy? We did no such thing. We simply retrieved the missing part of our vessel that was buried under your little town. We are going to send you back, we just needed you to come out of hiding. Is there more of you?' He asked. He looked a little confused about what they meant by destroy.

'There is no use in sending us back, our world is burned. It is ash. You burned it the day your bright ship arrived in the sky,' George explained. Izazon looked completely perplexed. *Does he not know what had happened?* James asked himself. There was another moments silence as the Ocularits spoke amongst themselves, in a tone which was not human.

'This really is a tragedy. I assure you this was not supposed to happen. I do *not* know how it did happen. I can one hundred percent say that it was not my orders,' he said.

There was a noise from behind the group. Blistrix came in through the doors.

'But you did do it Father. Can you not remember? Is your age getting to you?' Blistrix said to the high emperor.

'What is the meaning in your fantasy speech?' He said, then spoke to him in a different dialect, but was struck by Blistrix to speak only in a language the scared onlookers could understand.

'You did this,' Izazon said to his son. Blistrix did not reply, his eye darted around the room.

Jane noticed that the other Ocularits in the room were beginning to get a little unsettled and they tried to intervene.

'This council needs to take action against our ageing emperor. He has caused a planet to burn and millions of people died. You know as well as I do that the penalty is death,' Blistrix said to the other two Ocularits standing on the sidelines, they were the council they all presumed. They looked as though they needed to do something, but they did not know what to do. They spoke together for a while. Then the room fell silent.

'It is this council's decision to hold you Izazon, Just whilst we investigate these allegations, as you know we take these matters seriously. Wiping out a whole planet is an extreme case. Please can you follow us,' one of the two Ocularits said. Then they walked out holding Izazon by the arms. The doors closed on the room, everyone scared about what was going to happen next. Blistrix walked confidently to the door and locked it using a keypad to the right.

'Well. Now that fool has been taken care of. We can get on with more pressing matters. We have a revival to prepare,' Blistrix announced to everyone.

'Did you do this?' James asked.

'Of course I did. I wiped out your whole planet. Humans are like vermin, they need to be taken care of. I will take care of you all. First though, I need to complete the preparations. Please bear with me just a moment,' he said. As if they could move anyway, they were all so scared and worried about what might happen. He called over to someone in the corner. Out of the shadows walked Nadia.

'You cow,' Sharon said. 'What have you done with Alex?' she added. Nadia laughed at her questions and carried on with a variety of instructions given to her.

'We need one more sacrifice,' Nadia said. 'Any volunte-,' she managed before a spike was shafted into her body. It went through her back and came out of her stomach, it created a fountain of red.

'I'm sorry Nadia, well… not really. I don't need you anymore. You have done your job well and now it is time for me to shine,' Blistrix said. He started to cackle like a witch. Sounding almost hysterical. He twisted the spike around, causing Nadia to vomit, a mix of green vegetation and bile fell from her lips, making a pool on the floor. The others had to hold their noses as this happened, the smell was almost unbearable. They would have ran out screaming but they were transfixed on what was going on. Jane had to cover her eyes, she felt sick herself, as did the others.

Blistrix pressed a button on his wrist. It made the floor rumble under their feet and then the floor opened up. It looked like a secret trapdoor. There was something inside. He pulled a test tube item from his gown and filled it with blood dripping from Nadia, then pushed her lifeless body to one side.

'This is what I've been waiting for. All I needed were more dirty humans to complete the sequence. It is now complete. Rise from the ground and let us begin the revival,' as he spoke, there was something coming from the floor and up into the Chamber room. It looked like a large fish tank. 'Now the human race with be eliminated,' he said, laughing as the tank steadily rose higher and higher, entering the room in which they all stood.

Chapter 17

The mysterious tank rose higher and higher into the room at a steady pace, the ground beneath them vibrating slightly as it did so. All of them were staring at it with complete attention. There was nothing that could break this mesmarisation. Nora had a feeling run through her body when what was inside revealed itself.

'Introducing, Experiment 126,' Blistrix announced. 'We have been experimenting on you humans for some time now, but this one... this one was different. This specimen knew about us. It knew of my intentions. Very clever little thing really. I have been keeping it, to study the intelligence. We have been monitoring the thoughts, feeling and memories of this one.'

The tank rose higher. It became clear to the onlookers that it was a woman. She was naked inside what looked like water, but turned out to be something else entirely. The woman had wires connected to her head and some other parts of her body. These wires lead under the floor where they were standing. She reminded James of something he had seen once in a movie, it made all those movies he had watched just part of his normal life now. He could not believe that all this existed and now there he was standing in the unreal setting. It hit him all at once that he needs to be ready for whatever life threw at him.

'Beautiful isn't it. It is the only one I have grown to like. This one has a greater intellect than any other. I needed five human sacrifices to regenerate this experiment, it's almost complete. When Nadia and the others arrived I was quick to snap up two of their crew. It gave me great pleasure to deal with those ones, they were fiery. Nadia then helped me with my work, she has done a brilliant job,' Blistrix explained. 'When I successfully destroyed your planet, I had to be careful as I needed some more sacrifices.'

The tank rose higher still, revealing the experiment's abdomen and top of her thighs. Nora stared, there was something about her that she noticed. Something that seemed so familiar.

'Shelly?' She muttered under her breath. 'Shelly is that you?' Nora saw that it was her great, great aunt Shelly White. Everything started to fall into place in her mind. She understood now why they couldn't find her in her room at the asylum, all those years ago. She had been taken by these monsters.

'I wondered how long it would take you to notice,' Blistrix said. 'Believe me, you being here is only coincidental. She had a gift that we needed to research. We knew you two were of the same bloodline,' he added. His eye focused on Nora as she approached the tank cautiously. The tank still rising.

'How does it feel to see her?' Blistrix said and then let out a brief laugh. 'Shame you two won't have long, when she awakes I will finally find out how she knew what she knew and then I will have no use for her anymore. I will let her die as I will with you filthy creatures.'

'H-How is this possible. Is she still alive?' Nora asked.

'For now, that liquid she is in is a preservative. When it drains she will have a little while then she will die. Marvelous isn't it. There is nothing more satisfying than watching a human wriggle and dry up in front of your eyes. It does give me thrills,' he laughed.

He walked around to the back of the tank and pulled open a drawer. Inside it was four vials of deep red blood. The fifth, Nadia's, he had in his hand.

The survivors looked upon what he was doing.

They did not know whether to run or wait. Though with the door to the room locked, they knew that they would not get very far. They could hear a beeping sound, Blistrix was pressing buttons on a keypad. There was then a loud siren sound in the room, it echoed and rang in their ears. James covered his ears and stood by his mother. Sharon grabbed George and could no longer hold back her tears. Blistrix came to the front of the tank again.

'Shall we begin?' he looked upon everyone. Even though he did not have a mouth, they knew he was smiling an evil grin. The kind of grin every villain in every movie does at one point or another.

Chapter 18

It felt as if the walls were pulsing around them all. It thudded in their ears, a regular beat. To some it felt like they were submerged in water and the sound was of their own heart beating in their ears.

All the survivors huddled closer together as the sound continued. It was almost unbearable. To accompany the bass of the beating, a beeping sound could be heard coming from the tank, an ear piercing sound, like a scream from an animal in pain.

The tank which was now acting as the center piece to the room was beginning to drain of its life-preserving liquid, though it was only draining slowly. Blistrix did not seem to notice, he was watching the others with his; haunting, ever watchful eye.

The thudding noise was still audible, almost forcing Sharon to cover her ears, but by the look she had on her face, it was not helping. She looked around at her fellow survivors and could see that they were all in a trance, looking as the tank slowly emptied, it reached the top of Shelly's head and started to go down past her face, as it did the remaining water dripped off of her nose and chin.

'What is going to happen?' Nora asked.

'When the tank is empty, she will then reveal the secrets of her all seeing ways. The specimen will tell me how she had come to see the future. Then I will simply kill off what life she has remaining,' once again they could all feel that smile, though it was not visible. 'Oh, before I kill you too Nora, I want to thank you.'

'Thank me...for what?'

'For showing me around that town of yours.' He looked towards Nora who took a step back. For a second she had to think about what he was talking about, then it clicked.

'You. You overtook my body. You caused my blackouts. You were the voice inside my head all along,' she was remembering back to when she thought she was going insane, waking up randomly in the 'Hill's Angel' and the other house in town. She remembered the massive headache she had constantly. She remembered seeing something in her bedroom. It was him. She had a feeling that the voice sounded so familiar.

'It was fascinating.'

'What exactly were you looking for?'

'Well I wanted to know more about the place where this specimen came from, also to see what sacrifices I could play with,' he laughed as he said the last few words. It was demonic. Nora did not reply to this, she seemed like she was in shock. Sharon held her tight, a faint feeling overcame her. She went as white as a sheet and stumbled a little backwards. Nora had nothing else to say, her head looked down towards the ground.

'We are all that was left?' Jane asked.

'You were indeed. There was no one else in town at the time of disembarkation,' he explained.

'What about Father Michael? He wouldn't have just left the town. He wanted to make sure people were safe.'

Blistrix laughed. It echoed through all their ears.

'I took care of him personally, with a little help from the late Nadia. I made her lure him out into the heat. It didn't take him long to die, I was surprised.'

No one else said anything. It was silent apart from the thudding sound, which reminded them all that this was actually happening. James looked up towards the tank which was now half empty. He was sure it wouldn't be long before it would run dry. They all looked towards it with fear and fascination. Still the thudding noise persisted. A single tear ran down Nora's eye as she watched her great, great aunt behind the glass. She had not known her personally, only through the stories that had been told. She remembered being fascinated by this woman who was now in front of her. A tear emerged as her mind recalled her mother, how she used to talk about how crazy Shelly was, that they locked her up in the Merryville Asylum for the mentally insane. She remembered how she felt about this woman; *was Aunt shelly crazy?* As she saw the liquid drain from around her body, she didn't think so, not anymore. Not now that the truth was known.

The water continued to trickle and it was now past Shelly's waist. With the water running out, everyone noticed how many wires were actually connected to her.

'Where do those wires go?' George asked. Blistrix looked at him, concerned as he did not know the answer. They could all see through his eye expression that he didn't have a clue. He searched quickly for an answer.

'I have people that do all this heavy work for me. I have the fun of the kill,' he said. George noticed that that grin filled the air again.

The water was now at knee level. Mark saw that it would not be long before they all met their end. His palms felt clammy as he stood there with the others. *What more can I do?* He thought to himself. So he just continued to watch as the water emptied, past her knee and down her shin.

Sharon held Nora, who was trying hard to keep her emotions a secret. Sharon now had to become the person her husband had been; strong, confident and she felt like she had to be there for Nora. A burden that she did not mind one bit. The hairs on the back of her neck stood to attention as the last of the liquid ran dry from the tank and a nauseating sound could be heard, like oil down a plug hole. It sounded almost like it was bubbling.

They waited.

They watched.

The wires that were connected to Shelly started to change colour, from their neutral grey, to red, green and blues. They were bright, like neon. They illuminated Shelly's vacant face like a rainbow. The colours started changing from one to another, it reminded James of their Christmas tree, fiber optic lights. He wondered in that moment whether he would ever see his Christmas tree again, he thought maybe not.

The illuminated wires continued their light show, as Blistrix pressed one final button. A burst of air escaped the tank with a high pitched screech. They all covered the ears and grimaced at the sound. Then there was silence. Too intrigued about what might happen next, all their eyes were transfixed on the tank.

Chapter 19

Amazed and scared beyond belief, they all looked at each other in puzzlement. Blistrix was wandering around the tank looking at all the wire connections. Then a sound could be heard, very slight, but it was definitely there.

A beat... then another... then another. A heartbeat. It was beginning to thud faster and faster until it was at a normal human rate. The lights stopped changing colour. They just glowed, constant and vibrant.

Her eyes began twitching. She looked like she was waking up for the first time. It was emotional almost, to watch as this fully grown woman was seemingly seeing the world for the first time, seeing the colours and hearing the sounds. Her eyes opened wider, they seemed to be adjusting to the light which flooded the room. She looked like she was trying to focus. Though her eyes seemed to take a while. Slowly and cautiously looking around, Shelly could feel everyone staring at her, but she could not bring herself to see them clearly yet.

Her mouth, twitching on one side, trying to open up. She managed to open her lips a little, then closed them shortly after this revelation. Shelly tried again and again, each time opening her mouth a little more, skin creasing around her lips. Again her muscles tried to open her mouth. Everyone looking at her like a sideshow attraction at a circus, her senses were ripe and she felt like her body could do this. Strange voices intruded her head, it was like she could hear everyone's thoughts. *Go on,* one thought intruded in her brain. *She can't do it,* another said. It occurred to Shelly after a few more of these ramblings that she was in fact reading their thoughts. She could not begin to pin point whose thoughts were whose, she was still in a daze and confusion shadowed everything else.

Her eyes adjusted more, she could see all those who were staring upon her. She caught a glimpse of something beside her... Blistrix. He was looking upon her, with triumph. The secret he had kept from Izazon and the council, had finally been revived.

Shelly looked upon him, not with fear, but with confusion. *What is she going to say?* A thought entered her mind from one of the onlookers. She began to feel more strength in her muscles and managed to say something. Just audible.

'W- Where am I?' Though this was a direct

question, no one replied to her. She continued to scan the room and did not seem to notice anyone in the crowd. Her eyes were now fully functional and her movement was beginning to kick in more and more each second.

'Where am I?' She pleaded again.

'You are in another universe,' Blistrix replied. Nora looked as though she was about to say something but Blistrix was too intimidating, she was not brave enough to talk, she refrained from speaking.

Shelly did not look surprised by this reply. She just continued to take in her surroundings. Her strength was enough to move her hand up in front of her and she examined it with wonder, like she was seeing it for the first time. She then looked at her sides and her shoulder and saw the wires protruding from her skin.

'What do you want from me?' She asked. It broke the onlooker's hearts to hear how much worry and longing was inside her voice. Sharon, Nora and Jane had tears rolling down their flushed cheeks.

'I demand that you tell me how you knew about us, long before we arrived in Merryville,' Blistrix said. Shelly looked confused about what the demand was. She was not aware of anything that she may or may not know. She tried to remember back to a time when she was a young girl, but her mind put up a wall. The more she tried to think, it hurt her head.

'I...I don't know... what you mean,' she said to him.

'You better think. You do not have long left before you expire,' he explained to her.

She tried so hard to remember back, she could not recall what he was talking about. Her mind was a muddle of words and letters, scrambling about inside her brain. A few minutes passed and there was no further information. Blistrix looked as though he was starting to lose his patience.

'I'm waiting, human,' he said sternly, it reminded James of some of his teachers in school, the way he said it. Shelly just managed the energy to shrug at this statement. 'Let me remind you shall I?' He said. 'A long time ago, you somehow began to receive messages from us. I do not know how and I do not know what. I do not care. You were then locked up by some fellow humans. They said you were dangerous and needed care. They locked you up in the Merryville Asylum...' he continued.

Blistrix carried on with his story, but Shelly had some kind of memory flood at those last words. The asylum, she can remember laying on the bed and staring at the ceiling. She remembered it was dinner time and the orderlies had brought round a questionable meal for her to eat. It was left untouched. She remembered something standing in the corner, looking at her. Her memories presented to her, the blackout she had experienced, then waking up in some alien place. So many pictures were invading her brain at the same time. A feeling of fear and exhaustion presented itself as the images and words were flashing in her mind like a flipbook. Her breath was caught. She could suddenly see all the areas of the vessel they were now in. She could see all the rooms at the same time, like her body was some sort of security camera hub. It was like looking into another world, she could not begin to describe it if she tried. The images were still flying through her mind.

More memories were presenting themselves to her, she could remember someone holding her down.

'Don't worry,' the voice said to her. 'When you wake up you will be able to see everything. You will know what to do with this information,' the voice continued. A picture in her head was of an Ocularit with a purple gown and green gloves. Her memory shifted onto another Ocularit that was present. This one wearing a similar attire. Her memories drifted, she again could see all the rooms in the ship. She could see Blistrix and a girl talking. She could see Blistrix killing some other humans, then another. Shelly was certain that at any moment her head was just going to blow up from all the information. Then her memory shifted back to when she was being held down on a cold metal table.

'We are rigging you up to the central core system. You will be able to see and remember everything that happens on this ship. I know that Blistrix is up to something. I can hear him planning something with one of the guards,' the other voice said to her.

It was all becoming a clear picture in her mind. The pictures inside her head were slowing down, as her mind tried to organise them all.

'When he wakes you up, make sure everyone on board knows about what he is planning. I fear that there is a planet at stake here.'

Suddenly, all at once, she could see all.

Chapter 20

'You planned all this long ago. You started planning your attack on Earth long before I got here. You and another one of your people. That girl you killed was in on it too,' Shelly was saying.

'This is not news. I am intrigued about how you know this though,' Blistrix said to her, moving closer to the glass.

'I see all. These wires lead all around this vessel. I can see every room and every corridor. I know all the conversations that have happened here.'

Shelly could see that Blistrix was not happy about this revelation.

'You wanted the burning of the Earth to look like Izazon's doing. Your own father. Just so you could become High Emperor yourself. The council were on to you before all this though. They were the ones that wired me up, to expose your deed,' Shelly explained.

'Impossible. They should have executed Izazon

by now, for his heinous acts. Even if they have not, you have no way of telling them, you are nearly out of oxygen.'

'I have sent a message via the optical wire, which runs through to the Optical room and I have sent out the signal. Also I have sent a voice confession. They are on their way here this moment,' Shelly said. She smiled slightly at him. He looked at her with his eye and though his mouth was nonexistent, everyone could guess his expression.

A few moments went by, there was silence. The survivors were a bit confused about what was actually happening before their eyes. James thought, *last minute revelations only happen in the movies.* They all felt a little hope that they might not be killed after all. Though they did not know what the other Ocularits were like.

'This is impossible... impossible,' Blistrix mumbled to himself. He knew that he had been exposed to the council.

'There is no way they are going to make you high-emperor now,' Shelly said to a frustrated Blistrix.

A few seconds which felt like hours went by. There was a noise, a noise that was barely audible to begin with... footsteps. As the noise grew, it was clear to everyone that it was not just one pair of feet either.

The footsteps halted and the door struggled, but did not open.

'Open this door. This is your master, Izazon here,' the voice said.

'Ha. You will never catch me,' Blistrix said and went to the tank and pressed a sequence of buttons. The floor then began to open up. The room seemed to grumble slightly underfoot.

James ran over to the doors and pressed the button to open it. Izazon and the two members of the council came marching in, heading towards Blistrix.

'Blistrix, we find you guilty of all the accusations against you. You will be sentenced to death by incineration,' one of the council members announced. The floor was still opening up before them all.

'You'll have to find me first. Make sure you look over your shoulders. I am going to make sure I finish you all off,' he promised and plunged into the blackness that had opened up. His laugh could be heard as he fell all the way.

They all looked around the room, all felt deflated as their emotions and adrenaline ran through their bodies. Thoughts of home and Earth came back to them all. They all thought that the situation they were in was a dream. Then their senses came back, it reminded them that all of it was real. Mark looked upon the survivors and could not believe the treachery he felt towards Nadia. The Petersons huddled together. Sharon had puffy eyes and felt like she was going insane. Nora was admiring Shelly in the tank and Shelly looked into her niece's eyes, not knowing who she was.

Stunned, everyone was stood still, not knowing what was going to happen next. All that could be heard was the breath escaping their lungs and inhaling once again. They had all started to become used to their life onboard the vessel, but missed their homes more, their routines.

Blistrix was at large and they all knew what they had to do… fight! They all thought the same thought at the same time, *we need to fight.* It was what was needed. Though they all had no idea about how many more obstacles were in their path before they could feel safe again.

Entity III

Prologue

The night is cool. There's not a sound anywhere to be heard. It seems that they are the only ones in the world. They walk towards what promises to be a new life, a good life. The promise of a path of wealth and fame.

They clamber onboard and take their nearest seat. Then there is a sound, an alarm, quiet yet prominent in the still night. Mark, Nadia, Vincent, Thomas and Matt all sitting still and waiting for their dreams to begin. It had taken a long time for them all to get to this point in the mission, working all so hard for this day.

Through their headsets they could hear the countdown given from the ground control. It seems like the countdown is slow and Nadia and Mark look towards each other with both worry and excitement in their faces. Thomas and Matt seem to be none the wiser about what is about to happen, both are in their own little worlds, looking through the small windows of the craft to the world outside.

A rumble...

The rocket started to vibrate. They began to feel hot with nerves. Nadia grabbed hold of Marks hand as the rocket began to be propelled upwards. She looks behind at her fellow passengers and could see all their faces smiling towards her.

'Here we go boys... WOOOOOOO!'

The G-force made their faces feel tight, this only made them all laugh. They all thought that nothing could be better than this adventure they had just embarked on... yet!

*

Moments later they were weightless. They had entered zero gravity. The earth was still visible from the windows, how lonely the planet looked to them all. So many colours could be seen, not only blue from the oceans, but the different spectrum of green from the trees and landscapes. The situation hit them, they have begun their mission. They did not know when they would return to their homes. A tear rolled down Nadia's cheeks, as she looked upon the planet.

'Right. First thing is first. Vincent, you contact control and tell them it had been mission successful, we are in space. Matt, check over the craft for maintenance and any engineer work which may be needed after exiting Earth's atmosphere. Nadia and I will start to work on our journals, we need to make sure that we document everything. Thomas will overlook the rocket to make sure all is fine. Great work guys. This is it,' everyone did what was asked of them after Mark had finished his speech. All were high on the buzz of adrenaline which coursed through their bodies.

*

Over the next few days, then weeks that followed, they settled into their jobs. Though nothing could prepare them for what hardship was to lie ahead when they came face to face with the entity.

Chapter 1

'Trust... What is trust? You put your life into someone's hands. You tell them your life stories and pour your heart out. It just goes to show you that you can never tell a person's true intentions. A life without trust is no way to live. I feel cold, afraid and alone. We can all say that we trust each other, but do we? Do we *now*?' Sharon span her ring around her finger, thinking about Alex and the trust that they shared. She looked down towards the ground, never engaging eye contact or her fellow survivor's reactions. 'I said it once and I will say it again. Can we really trust each other now? Nadia, what she was capable of. She...' Sharon stumbled on her words, barely keeping herself together. Her words hung in the air like a deflating balloon.

Seeing she was on the verge of a breakdown, Nora put her arm around the upset Sharon, but she pulled away from the embrace. Still, she continued spinning the ring around her finger.

Nora recalled the look on her great aunt

Shelly's face as she was close to death, then again as the Ocularits stabalised her again inside her glass tank. The older lady felt a little better knowing that she had not died and that she was still there. It almost gave her something to fight for.

Across the grey room, Jane, George and James were huddled together, tired and hungry. They were drifting in and out of sleep, whilst listening to the monologue of a hurt woman. James' breathing was smooth and calming and he managed to fall asleep to the sound of his own breath. His parents both looked pale, emotionally exhausted from what had transpired.

It was not only Sharon that felt that the rope that held all of them together was gone. They all felt like they could not trust each other, though they knew they had to get through this situation. No one could think of anything to make themselves feel better. Frustrated, all the survivors contemplated their individual goals, then rested on their own thoughts.

'I remember Father Michael saying that trust is all we have,' Sharon started to recall. 'He said this the day after the light came down, he said we needed to stay together, not just me and Alex, but all the residents of Merryville. But I just don't know anymore,' she continued.

Nora remained quiet along with the others

whilst the words filled the room, echoing into every corner. She looked over towards the Petersons and she could physically see how much they had changed since the beginning. They all had vacant faces that did not show any emotions. The older woman scanned around the room in which they resided. She was unmoved by the all too familiar grey walls and ceiling. She was used to it, she agreed that it was a depressing sight to get used to but those were the facts. They all had called this place home for what felt like a lifetime. It seemed that gone were the happy memories. All that could be thought of was life on board the vessel.

Quiet was normal life for them all. The silence deafened their ears. The pain of acid rushing from their stomachs to their throat, a regular event.

'It's making me uneasy at how we did not spot her deception before it was too late. The worst thing is, I thought that there was something strange going on. I kept waking up to find someone entering and leaving the room. I did not pursue it though, as I thought it was Vincent on one of his sleepwalks. Maybe, if I pushed her with some more questions, she may have given up... I don't know,' Sharon looked up briefly and saw the depressing sights and quickly lowered her head again. The room went quiet as they all recalled the last few days. All thinking about what they could have done differently.

It felt to all of them, that they were all living on borrowed time. All knew that death could creep up on them at any moment.

'I wonder how Mark is getting on with his meeting with… those things. We need to hunt down Blistrix and get rid of him, then get rid of all the others. I bet they are all in on it. But at least if we get Blistrix I would feel a little bit less on edge in this unforgiving place. As a child I wished and dreamed about going into space. Now that I am here, well…' Sharon taped off with her own thoughts again.

It wasn't long before they were surprised by the brilliant white light that haunted the ship invaded their space. Sitting to attention, they all stared towards Mark, intrigued about what had happened and what was said.

Mark pulled up a chair and figured out in his head about where to start. He looked around the room and saw that he had everyone's attention. To the others, he looked like a child, scared and alone. He breathed heavy and then said a simple sentence which made all of them terrified.

'Well…its time…time to go to war.'

*

Nothing but silence was heard as the remaining humans walked out of the dull, gloomy room they had been resting within. They travelled down the monotonous hallways, bright with light. The bright lights which were once unbearable, now normal and frustrating.

One foot in front of the other they walked in a conga line like ants. They finally reached the Chamber. The doors to the huge room opened up revealing an empty space. Izazon and his two council members were facing the humans, their lone eyes darting around each of their faces, it was like they were reading them like books.

'Thank you for coming,' Izazon said in a haunting voice, none of the humans looked at him as he spoke, they focused their eyes on the ground at their feet. 'I know that this is an emotionally and physically exhausting time for you all but we need to come together as one. You must remember our race were just pawns in Blistrix's dastardly plans, we too have lost. I'm sure we can learn to trust again.'

'Ha,' Sharon laughed. 'It's that word again, trust. What does it mean, it's easy to say, not so easy to mean. How do we know you are not like...*him*?' She asked now looking directly into his eye. The Ocularits continued to look at all the humans. Izazon finally spoke, breaking the silence.

'I understand your distrust. How would you know if we were different than my son? I could say that we are, but its trust that will decide it in the end,' he explained.

The three Ocularits spoke amongst themselves in high and low squeaks and rumbles for a short time and then one went towards the back of the room.

'It goes without saying that we are all in danger here, with Blistrix on the run, who knows what he is capable of. One of my council will hand you a weapon to defend yourself with. Like a gun it will travel fast when triggered, though instead of killing him, it will comatose him for a short while,' Izazon explained.

'Why would you want him alive?' George asked, becoming annoyed at their way of dealing with the situation.

'I have my reasons, something that I have been pondering, all will be revealed in the end. Right, two groups of humans to split and go on the search,' he instructed.

The humans stared for a moment and then conversed a little. The Petersons in one group, leaving Nora, Sharon and Mark in the other.

'This ship is huge with higher and lower levels. One group start at the top and the other start at the bottom. I will disperse Ocularits Units from the center in both directions. If you see Blistrix, shoot him in the eye, he will then be in a stable coma, understood?' he asked and the humans nodded.

The groups were given protective armor and then lead by one of the council to an elevator. In all their minds they wondered if they would live to see another day.

*

<u>TechSPACE - Written Transmission #1</u>

```
We have spent the day travelling
through this marvelous space.
There are stars and a variety of
other things in our view. It is
strange, the stars do not look any
closer, only much brighter. Their
brightness is enchanting, absolute
perfection. I can imagine that
this is the feeling some people
get when they spend hours staring
at a fish in a tank. I'm not
ashamed to say that we have all
cried today, just from the
excitement and the overwhelming
sense of pride we feel. For some
of us it had felt like a distant
dream that would never come true,
so the fact that we are here is
```

literally a dream come true.

There are endless colours surrounding us. Blues, yellows and purples to name just a few, all are painted on a backdrop of the infinite black of space. It really is a sight to behold. This experience is everything I hoped that it would be and more. I can only anticipate that the further into space we delve, the more exhilarating the experience will be.

Our living conditions are good, basic but good. The minimalistic space that we are now going to spend the next couple of weeks only enhances the amazing views around us.

Everyone is happy with their assigned jobs and all is going smoothly and according to plan. I will try and update as much as possible. We know that what we have to do is record and report on all the things that we see, though if there is another job you need us to do whilst we are in this amazing place then please let us know.

Regards,

Mark Noir
Research Team Captain

Chapter 2

Their tongues were dry with anticipation and fear of what might be waiting for them. The Petersons were in one elevator going up, whilst the other survivors were going down to the bowels of the ship. The elevators were small and just about fit their groups. As the Petersons reached the top the others reached the bottom, the journey seemed long, they thought that maybe they were overthinking what outcomes may happen.

Mark stepped out into an empty, cold corridor which was much darker than the other corridors they had grown used too. Sharon stepped out next, followed by Nora. They all remained silent, as did the space around them. Nora noticed that there was a buzzing in her head, where it was so quiet. The walls were made from the same depressing shade of metal… Grey everywhere they looked.

'Which way shall we go?' Sharon asked, breaking the silence and making them all jump. It took a few seconds for their hearts to reach a normal beat again.

'I'm not sure,' Mark replied.

'Both ways look the same, its dark down here. It's unnerving,' Nora stated. They carried on the way they were going, though it seemed the further they went, the darker it got. All their eyes, struggling to focus, like a camera would trying to focus on an object in a dark space. It was not long before they reached a door and tried the handle, but it did not budge. Mark pressed his ear up against the door to hear for any movement. There was none, they moved on, delving further into darkness and the unknown.

*

'Well, it sure is different up here,' Jane said, stepping out of the elevator into a big room. The room was minimalistic, just like the rest of the ship. There was a humming noise which was coming from the corner. All three of the Petersons walked towards it and it looked like some sort of generator. Below was something written in a language they did not recognise.

'It must be *their* language,' James said, though he felt silly after he had because there is nothing else it could be, though no one really cared.

'Right, we need to make sure that we stick

together. We need to find this *monster*,' George said. By these words, they all suddenly felt more motivated and determined. They all walked towards the only exit from the room and as they did the door opened automatically. The corridor which greeted the Petersons was just as bright as the rest of the ship they had ventured around. The air felt light and the atmosphere was peaceful. There did not seem to be anything to panic about.

*

Their eyes slowly became adjusted to the dull light. Sharon had to squint at times and feel the walls as she walked. It was still so quiet, she felt like her heart was a drum being played in her ears. There did not seem to be any sign of life anywhere.

'Where do you think everyone is?' She asked.

'I have no idea, but you need to stop scaring me every time you talk. It's so quiet,' Nora replied.

'Sorry,' Sharon said.

'I think Izazon would have distributed all his available army, like he said. I feel like we can trust him. He and the other two members of the council seem to be ok, but still we must remain defensive,' Mark explained. The three of them continued to walk down the seemingly never ending corridor, searching for an opening they could investigate.

They stumbled across more doors, but none were accessible.

There was a smell which loomed in the air. It smelt like death, rotting flesh against the cold, seemingly rusted metal, though the thought of metal rusting in space was just bizarre. None of them conversed about it, it was just there.

*

'Did you hear something?' Jane asked the other two. Neither of them had heard a sound.

'What was it?' James asked. Jane shrugged her shoulders and signaled to carry on down the corridor. They came to an opening and there was someone or something standing in the middle looking at some sort of computer screen.

'Hello?' George called. The thing looked around, they were stupidly relieved that it was not the Ocularit they had been looking for. They did not feel ready to fight just yet, they were intrigued by the layout of the ship and wanted to explore and get used to the new levels that have been revealed to them.

'Hello. You must be Jane, George and James. Izazon told me about you. He mentioned that you would be exploring the upper levels in search of Blistrix. My name is Luvax, I take care of the injured and sick,' the new acquaintance explained.

'Have you seen any sign of Blistrix?' Jane asked.

'No. I'm afraid not. I doubt if he would come here. He knows my overwhelming loyalty to the High Emperor and the council. Though I suppose you never know with him, he is…' he stopped and looked both ways. 'Evil,' he concluded.

'Is there anyone else on this level?' James asked.

'There are quite a lot of rooms, the same as all the other levels of this vessel. Though all the rooms that are locked are not accessible unless you have the emperors key, which he has at all times, so it would be a waste of time trying to enter any of those rooms. You can come back anytime you need whilst you're looking. I'll be here anticipating patients from the impending conflict.'

'What impending conflict?' George asked.

'You don't really think Blistrix is on his own do you? He has loyal Ocularits all over this ship. Be vigilant and do not say anything unless you have too.' Luvax explained. The hearts of George, Jane and James all sank in their chests at the prospect of others like him around. They turned and walked back out into the corridor, leaving Luvax watching his many computer screens.

*

Sharon was walking behind Nora and Mark. She ran up behind Nora, she could not shake the feeling of being watched, though there didn't seem to be anyone around.

'What is the matter with you girl?' Nora asked.

'I think there is something down here with us,' she replied. They stopped and looked around to where they had just come from. Silence was still present, then it was gone with an almighty bang. It made their hearts race so fast in their chests. Marks palms went instantly clammy with fear and Nora started shaking.

'W-Who's there?' Mark called out to the dark corridor they had just trekked.

'Hahahaha,' in the distance. 'I can see you. I'm coming to get you. You better run.' Just then an echo of a laugh could be heard coming from somewhere that seemed so far away but yet so close at the same time.

*

TechSPACE - Written Transmission #3

Following our conversation, I have sent some of our photographic findings. There seems to be more of the same sights at the moment. Though it is still beautiful and exciting, it would be nice to come across something more. Maybe I'm just being greedy wanting more, this place, space, is like a whole new world. I think that we all feel like we are in a dream and at any moment we are going to wake up.

We have now been up here for a few days and our attentions are still fully on the tasks at hand. We cannot see any major planets at the moment. I'm sure we will see the next planet on the horizon soon though. Thomas, Matt, Nadia and Vincent are all working on their goals and I am still working on mine also. I thought that I would just write down these ramblings. I feel like whilst I'm up here it is a good opportunity to report it live so I don't forget anything, it will be a nice keepsake of our adventure.

Right, duty calls, there is still so much to get done. Must get back to work now. Until next time.

ENTITY: THE COMPLETE TRILOGY!

Regards,

Mark Noir
Research Team Captain

Chapter 3

George looked around towards Jane and gazed deeply into her eyes. She wondered what he was doing. For a moment it took her back to the moment when they first met, when their eyes caught each other's across the crowded bar.

'Why are you looking at me like that?' She asked.

'I just had the most bizarre feeling. I wonder how the others are getting on.' He pondered.

'I don't know. I hope they find him and all this can be over. But then thinking about what Luvax said, Blistrix has others on board. This is going to be a long struggle.' James just remained quiet through all their conversing, looking left and right with a keen eye. The Petersons continued down the apparently never ending hallway, looking behind the doors that were open on the way.

*

'W-who's there?' Mark called. He felt his hands become instantly clammy. His lips were drying as he was talking. He felt that at any second something could happen, so he prepared himself. There was no answer to his question. He licked his lips and gums trying to speak again, though nothing came out.

'I do *not* like this at all,' Nora said and Sharon agreed. Mark retraced their footsteps a little.

'Hello?' He managed to call out to the cryptic voice, still there was no answer, though something could be heard. It took the trio a little time to figure out what it was.

Footsteps.

The footsteps were getting louder and so he rejoined the scared women he had left behind and they were about to make a run for it when Izazon could be heard calling towards them.

'Wait. Why are you running? Why do you look so scared?' He asked.

'We just heard something. A voice, sinister and threatening. We thought that maybe it was… *him*,' Sharon explained with a shaky voice.

'Hmmm, I did not hear anything. I will send some of my army to investigate.'

'I thought you guys were starting from the middle?' Mark asked, suddenly becoming very unnerved by Izazon's presence.

'We were. Our systems went down. We keep all our backup equipment and booster generators down here maybe that is what you had heard. I think maybe Blistrix is messing around, trying to scare us.'

'Well he is succeeding,' Sharon admitted.

'Stay on guard and everything will work out OK in the end. Trip up though and there is no telling what he might do… Also just stay vigilant of other Ocularits, I'm sure he is not working alone,' he warned them and then he turned and walked back the same way he came. The three of the humans resumed with the path they were investigating, even more scared at the thought of *others.*

*

George pushed on the remaining door on the current level they were exploring. The door needed a push but opened fully after the third shove. The room revealed a variety of archiving, they assumed that's what it was. They looked at a box, but could not understand any of the symbols, but inside were old documents. Documents that were faded with age and fragile to the touch.

'Well, I suppose we need to go down to another level. He isn't anywhere here,' James said.

'I agree. I cannot believe how quiet it is here. We have only seen one Ocularit since we started searching,' Jane said. George agreed also and the threesome walked back down the hallway to the elevator. Jane peeked in on Luvax, but he was no longer in sight.

*

'I feel so jumpy now after hearing that voice,' Sharon stated.

'Me too, but we just need to stay focused. I think we found an entrance we can explore,' Mark said. There was indeed an arch which lead to a spacious and bare room. In the room was a projector of some description.

'This is a weird place for a projector isn't it?' Sharon asked.

'Yes it is indeed. I wonder why it is down here. Unless it is *his*,' Nora said. Mark approached it with a little caution and pressed the only button on the box. What played was videos of Nora's aunt Shelly when she was in Merryville Asylum. The videos were plagued with misdeeds and the abuse that she suffered from her "caregivers". All of them looked at the video, completely shocked at what they were seeing. Then there was an eye which appeared instantly onscreen, making Sharon and Nora jump.

On closer inspection they could tell it was Blistrix. He was in the room with Shelly as she was sleeping then all of a sudden there was a bright light and then there was nothing occupying the room. Shelly just disappeared. Then the video clip ended.

'He obviously didn't want this CCTV to get out to the public,' Mark assumed.

'Indeed. It is vicious what they were allowed to get away with,' Nora said. 'It might sound silly but I'm glad Blistrix took her away from all that.'

'I would be too,' Sharon said. She put her arm around Nora for a second, just for that little bit of comfort, a lone tear rolled down Nora's face and dropped to the floor.

*

The Petersons exited the elevator to the lower level. It looked almost identical. The doorways were all in the same places and it was still so quiet. But then a voice could be heard coming from one of the closer rooms. It was the Ocularits language. George went to investigate, but the room which housed the voice a moment ago stood empty.

'I'm getting creeped out. This place just messes with your mind. It looks the same as the level we have just left. We can hear voices. Please tell me I am not going crazy,' Jane said.

'You're not hun, it's alright. We will be alright', George tried to reassure his scared wife.

'Shhhh… listen,' James interrupted.

A voice.

'Hello. How's the search going? I hope you are enjoying this game of cat and mouse. It is thrilling,' it was Blistix's voice. It was being played through some unseen speakers. 'Just to let you know your friends are doing really well. They are very jumpy, it is fun to watch.'

'Where are you?' George called out.

'At the moment I am just about to slaughter one of them. I can see them oh so very clearly from where I'm standing. They do not even know I am here. Let's see… which one to pick, it might be fun to leave the female counterparts alone.'

'Do not touch him, you animal,' James called.

'Threats won't do boy. Don't worry your time will come.'

'Please don't do this,' Jane called out. But there was no reply.

*

TechSPACE Written Transmission #5

We have just seen the most wonderful sight of our journey so far. It was a rock formation, though the space around it was so colourful, there were all the colours I have ever known, even some that I had never seen before. All the colours were swirling gently around the rocks, which were themselves dancing in the backdrop of black space. The only way that I can describe it is being underwater, seeing everything in a sort of slow motion form. I have said it before, but this is enchanting. I gave the others a day to enjoy the sights today so we could all take in as much as we could.

I hope you received our amazing images, we are still eagerly waiting for a response. The pictures are so beautiful and need to be shared with the world. This has made me so excited about what we may come across next.

Regards,

Mark Noir
Research Team Captain

Chapter 4

The room felt suddenly much colder than it did just a few moments before.

'Something isn't right here,' Sharon stated, becoming more nervous with every second that ticked past.

'I know, I almost get the feeling we are being watched,' Mark added, not making anyone feel better. Nora remained quiet, though she didn't think she could talk even if she had something to say. Her heart was beating like a drum in her chest. They all looked around trying desperately to see into the darkness of the room's corners, but were unable to.

'Come on, let's go. It's freaking me out,' Sharon said.

'Leaving so soon,' a voice said from somewhere close by. 'Just when it was about to get interesting.'

*

'We need to get to them George,' Jane said with urgency in her voice.

'It is probably too late. By the time we find a way down and then find them…' George tapered off, trying not to think about what might happen to Mark, Nora and Sharon.

'What now then?' Jane asked.

'We continue our search and hope that Blistrix is bluffing,' George suggested. Though they all knew what Blistrix was capable of and none held out much hope.

*

'Who's there?' Sharon shouted, knowing the answer already. 'If that's you, come out and surrender.'

'Don't you like our little game of hide and seek. I thought you humans loved it,' the haunting voice said. The air became colder still, Mark readied his hand on his blaster, ready to shoot when he appeared.

'Just come out, you silly thing,' Nora said, becoming annoyed and angry, her mind thinking back to the video they had seen of Shelly, her scared, isolated aunt.

Just then something moved in the shadows and without thinking Nora blasted a shot into the unknown darkness. The movement ceased after the loud bang that the shot made on impact. Nora felt sick in the depths of her stomach.

*

A light flickered just up ahead of the Petersons, they approached the area with caution. Underneath the flickering light was one doorway, the handle turned and the door opened revealing Luvax sat facing another computer screen.

'Oh,' Jane gasped. 'You made me jump.'

'Oh dear, we must not be so jumpy, any luck on your mission?' Luvax asked.

'No. None at all,' George said, sounding unknowingly defensive.

'Oh, that is a shame. I'm sure you are closer than you realise. This ship is big, but the areas unlocked are small. You're bound to come across him or one of his minions sooner or later,' he explained.

The Petersons were quiet as Luvax continued reassuring them that everything will work out.

*

'Someone is feeling brave aren't they,' Blistrix said, feeling amused. Nora's feeling of sick in her stomach continued, it raged and screamed at her. She had missed, all of them felt their chests go heavy with the tension that was weighing down the room. 'Anyway, I must be off, dastardly deeds await. You will see me sooner than you think. Or maybe one of my minions will greet you before.'

'Where are these minions?' Mark asked.

'Rest assured, I have Ocularits all over this ship. They work for the council and the emperor, but really they work for me and only me. I have Ocularits in the army, engineering, but my second in command is very important to me. I could not have got this far without him. You should visit him, he works in the infirmary. Ask for Luvax and tell him I sent you to get your death sentence.' Then the most demonic laughter filled the room and their heads, it echoed through the walls and then just like that, it was gone. The sickly silence reclaimed the room and all three of them stood like statues looking towards the open space before them.

*

<u>TechSPACE - Written Transmission #7</u>

```
I hope that you have been
receiving all our photo and video
updates, we have still not had any
```

replies. I suppose the fact we can still send these transmissions means that it must be going somewhere. We have reached a point in space where it is starting to look the same and are not sure how much further you need us to go. On our mission plan it says that we need to take pictures, record on our findings and send transmissions of our findings.

On behalf of myself and the others in my team please can you reply, just a little response so we know that our hard work is being reviewed by someone and not getting lost on the way. If you need me to send you anything again, then I have everything on the back up drive here on board.

Anyway, this week has been very exciting. It is amazing what colours can be found all the way out here. There are many different rock formations and debris that can be seen. Some even better than the ones we wrote about in a previous transmission. We have taken pictures of them all and will send them after I have finished typing this short report.

Again, I hope all is OK back on base.

Regards,

Mark Noir
Research Team Captain

Chapter 5

Luvax walked towards the Petersons and looked like he was about to say something, then stopped dead in his tracks. Jane looked over towards George who looked a little pale.

'Are you ok?' Jane asked. There was something in George's eyes that were not quite right.

'Sshhh,' George whispered. Barely audible. Luvax turned around and was working on his computer again. 'There is something not right with this one. He doesn't seem very concerned like the others.' Jane thought about the words he spoke, then recalled all the other conversations they had had with this *being*. The whole time he was so calm, unmoved by the ordeal. She felt her heart go heavy in her chest, the realisation that this creature in front of them could be just as dangerous as Blistrix caused her to shiver with fear slightly.

James stood by, analysing his surrounding very carefully, the way he has since they were brought on this ship. He was always a curious person, even as a child, he would look around and take in all that was around him. He used to recall his visits out to his mother carefully and with great detail. Then a noise broke the Petersons all out of their concentration. A loud beep sound, only lasting a few seconds.

'What was that?' Jane asked Luvax curiously.

'No need to worry. I have just had orders from my commander. We are moving into the next phase,' he said mysteriously.

'Who is your commander?' George asked, but there was no response immediately. There was just awkward silence between them all.

'What is the next phase?' Jane asked. At that question Luvax turned around and looked at them all with his one giant eye. Jane noticed that there was something different with him or maybe within him.

'I'm sorry,' he said walking towards them slowly. Jane and George involuntarily started walking backwards, James however stayed and stared at Luvax.

'James, we need to continue our search,' Jane said, signaling James to move.

'What is your rush, sit down,' Luvax said more welcoming, but there was something that underlined his hospitality… something darker.

'NO… thank you,' Jane said.

'Well, that is disappointing. I'm sure your youngling would like a snack,' he said becoming more sinister with every word he spoke. 'I've got all sorts of things for him to enjoy. He can have some lunch, or maybe I'll have him for lunch,' Luvax leapt forward and grabbed James with his long fingers. James tried hard to unleash the grasp, but couldn't. Jane and George moved forwards but a tunnel opened up beneath Luvax and James and they both were sucked in, leaving Jane and George now in an empty room, filled with nothing but scared emotions of what might happen next and what will happen to their cherished son.

*

'What the hell is going on here?' Nora asked. 'This is a maze and a game of cat and mouse. What the hell are we going to do?' she continued the ramblings, becoming more hysterical with every word she said.

'Calm down, calm down. Everything will be fine,' Mark tried to reassure the other two. 'We need to continue. For all we know he wasn't even in the room. He was probably using some sort of voice control system,' he tried to reason, but the other two weren't convinced.

A few moments later there was a rumble that was heard from above them. It sounded like a kettle as it was brought to the boil. The three of them looked up but did not move or say anything, there did not seem to be any need for any interaction, no one knew anything.

*

'What are we going to do George? He has our son. You knew there was something funny about him, I should have listened to you. We shouldn't have stopped. He is gone. I'm sure that it can only be bad what is happening to him,' Jane said frantically without taking a breath, thinking about all the terrible outcomes that may occur.

'Sssshhhh. We need to find them. If I get my hands on him I will rip that beady eye from his head,' George said.

'Oh my god, oh my god, oh my god. What are we going to do? I-,' Jane paused as the tears started to roll down her cheek. 'What if he's gone forever?' Jane collapsed to the floor, the energy and drive in her body escaping all at once. George knelt down beside her and pulled her body close to his. There was a warmth between both of them, but they had never felt so cold.

*

The rumbling continued and the sound got louder. Still puzzled by what the sound was the three of them searched the room slightly, but they did not find anything. They continued to look up at the ceiling of the cold, dark, metal room.

'I wonder what it is.' Sharon asked.

'I have no idea. Could be anything in this place,' Mark said. Just as he finished speaking, a hole in the ceiling opened up and Mark moved under it to find out the source of the mysterious rumbling sound. It all went quiet for a moment or two, their hearts could be heard, echoing throughout the room. They were sure that their heads would explode it was so quiet.

'I can't see any…,' they were the last words Mark Noir said. Just then a beam of light shone on him. He was stuck like a statue in its rays, then his face started to change, become redder and his head was sweating. His clothing began to singe with the incredible power of the heat. Mark caught fire and exploded, creating a loud bang which rang in Sharon and Nora's ears for minutes after. The two ladies screamed as their faces were splattered with the smoldering remains of their companion. Sharon could taste the blood in her mouth and up her nose. A sickly taste of burned iron. Nora removed her glasses and could see only red. For a second she could recall the moment when she was sat in her house and the red light invaded the town of Merryville, like she was seeing the world through rose tinted glasses. A sound brought her back… it was Blistrix.

'Got ya. Let's see how you do without your partner to guide you through. Remember I'm always watching. I can see everything. Which one will be next?' Then there was a slight laughter which ran in the air, barely audible, but definitely present.

*

<u>TechSPACE Written Transmission #9</u>

Still we have not heard a thing. We still wait for a response. I have told the others to stop with their missions for now. We are working so hard to get the research needed to carry on, but without a reply to our messages it seems like it is all for nothing. Though we are still enjoying the amazing sights there is a slight worry that is felt by all of us.

We should have enough supplies and

resources for a while yet out here. We will spend our days devising a plan to get back to base. I feel that, as a captain, it is my duty to abort this mission and bring us all back. I still class this mission as a success due to the amount of pictures, videos and reports we have. All of us have enjoyed the time we have spent up here, though we all feel that there is still so much more to explore, but maybe in the future we can reinvestigate

I just hope that we can be in contact before we make our home trip.

Regards,

Mark Noir
Research Team Captain

Chapter 6

Everything felt cold and dark. Alone without any other help, they felt like their lifeline had just disappeared. Nora looked at the remains of Mark, but did not dare say anything about what just happened before their eyes. Sharon was wiping away a blood splatter on her face when the sound of someone running was heard.

The two ladies looked up to see Izazon and the two other council members coming towards them with a small army of Ocularits behind them. Nora and Sharon tried to speak, tried to explain what had just happened, but it was no good. Sharon cried and Nora was just stood like a statue.

'I won't ask what has happened here,' one of the council members said. They weren't sure which one, both wore purple robes with green lining, covered in a material which looked like plastic.

'What are we going to do emperor?' asked the other council member. Not only did the two Ocularits look the same, the two voices sounded similar and without mouths it was guess work. Izazon looked upon everyone with a grand gesture he signaled the army to continue their search.

'What shall we do now? We can't carry on without Mark,' Sharon barely managed.

'I have every faith in you both, but due to the situation I think we should regroup and think of another plan,' Izazon said.

The emperor, followed by the council members and then Sharon and Nora exited the hallway into the elevator. Nothing more was said, though they all thought about what else they could say.

*

'Maybe we should go back to where we started. We need to tell someone about this. Hopefully someone can help. Maybe Mark will know where they take people, he has been on this ship the longest,' Jane said, trying to bring herself together and think of something helpful.

'Let's go back then. Like you said maybe someone else can help. I have a feeling thought that this is going to get worse before it gets better,' George said.

The two remaining Petersons walked helplessly back to the elevator, with one less person they felt defeated and devastated. As the elevator moved back down towards The Chamber they held each other close, in fear of losing one another.

*

'Ahhh, glad you came back,' Izazon said to Jane and George as they entered the familiar setting of The Chamber. 'We were going to send someone to find you. Are you missing someone?'

Jane felt her chest go heavy and fresh tears teased her eyes. She looked to George to say something, though there was no need.

'That is a shame. Both groups have lost a body. Mark and James. I could not have thought Blistrix could have been capable of something like this, I guess you never really know someone. He was my only son and still I had no clue what he is capable of. I have decided to keep us all together. My army is continuing their search and I feel that in light of the incidents and loss that has occurred, we need to remain here, in this room.'

'Are we just giving up then? What about James?' Jane shouted, it echoed from all the walls.

'Not giving up, no. Just being more careful. I don't want to lose more of you. Plus Nora and Sharon mentioned something about others. More of my Ocularits are working for Blistrix.'

'Luvax took James,' George said bluntly.

Even without facial features they could feel the look of confusion and shock horror coming from Izazon.

'My Luvax? That has rattled me, though I recently had a disagreement with him. He is probably doing it from spite. It makes me feel better about James though, I do not think Luvax is capable of killing someone. Though if his loyalty towards Blistrix is great...' he tapered off, thinking about the mess of the situation.

The room went quiet. Jane and George didn't feel any better from Izazon's words, but they had to trust what he was saying, that maybe there was a little hope. The four remaining humans eventually slumped to the ground in exhaustion. They were all so tired. Sleep was kind and soon caught up with them.

*

<u>TechSPACE Written Transmission #10</u>

Mark doesn't know I am writing this transmission. Everyone is asleep and I thought it was a good opportunity.

Please, if there is anyone there reading these pages, please contact my family to say where I am. Please tell them if anything happens to us out here. The addresses and contact details are in my personal folder back at base.

Please get back to us,

Nadia Trott
Research Team, Second in Command

Chapter 7

The door opened loudly and they all looked around to see who it was. Jane and George sat hoping to see James walk in, but it was not. They wondered how long they had been in The Chamber, it felt like days, but realistically was only a few hours. The silence their ears had become used to again broken by the sound of a few Ocularits walking in unison to the high emperor to give an updated report. Though it was not good news for the Petersons. James had been found, lifeless and alone in a dark room. The Ocularits had laid James out in one of their disused rooms, they said that Jane and George should not look in at him though, as the damage done by Blistrix and Luvax made James unrecognisable. The information the Ocularit said to Izazon was vague and Izazon did not want to press for more information as he could see that Jane and George was looked at them anxiously. A note of some kind was handed to the high emperor, the inscriptions were alien to the humans, though Jane and George did not care about any note, they had lost their most precious possession. Jane's eyes were instantly filled with tears, which eventually she could not hold in. George held her hand and squeezed, trying to stay strong, but still he struggled with his own grief.

The note, the high emperor explained said; TuUyT, translated meant, "to be continued". He explained that the language used was not one that they practiced very much in their times. The language is that of an old cult group which worshiped their equivalent to the devil and they summoned spirits and dark forces to help them predict the future. The humans found it all too much to take in, it all seemed so far-fetched that their minds did not process the information given.

'So they used to think that these spirits made you psychic?' Nora asked. The others looked at her.

'Something along the lines of that. It goes much deeper. They thought that having these psychic abilities gave you the power to change your future. It does get much more complicated but I will not bore you with these details right now,' Izazon said, as he looked over to see Jane and George cuddling each other.

'Do you think that was why he wanted Aunt Shelly? He said something about her being able to predict his plans. I can't quite recall it. I think that she was a little psychic, that's why they sent her away to the asylum.'

'It does seem possible and it adds up that way. He must have studied the group a long time. Right now though I think our own group is suffering. We have lost too much time already, let's not lose anymore. Your friends need you to comfort them.'

Nora and Sharon gingerly approached the Petersons and knelt down beside them. The four neighbors held each other and sobbed hopelessly together. To mourn the loss of their youngest Merryville survivor.

*

<u>TechSPACE Written Transmission #16</u>

```
We were on course to return to
base but the engine has stopped,
it just went completely silent. I
looked at the control and the
manual but there does not seem to
be an explanation. On top of that
the craft if floating further away
from where we want to be heading.
We will soon be heading into
uncharted territory.

This is officially an S.O.S call.
If anyone is there, please find a
```

way to communicate to us. We need more information about how to get this ship back to Earth.

Please!

Mark Noir
Research Team Captain

Chapter 8

Sharon found herself staring at Jane and George, knowing the loss they must feel. She constantly thought about Alex and the love and joy he brought her. Her mind drifted back to happier memories, of them both growing up together. It brought a hint of a smile to her face. Her mouth almost hurt as the smile formed upon her face as it had been so long.

Jane looked into space, not knowing what to do or say. Her eyes, like George's, were red, bloodshot and puffy. They both felt like their tears had dried and that they would not be able to cry anymore. Their minds were numb, unable to think, unable to function properly. Both in a state of raw shock, their energy gone. George fell in and out of sleep, Jane remembered past birthdays and Christmas's, though her mind kept coming back to the moment he was taken from them. Then the headache started, her body could not take thinking about it any longer. She sighed as she put her head into George's lap and looked into nothingness. Just staring at the wall on the opposite end of the room at the common grey colour they had been haunted by. Her head was rested upon James' jumper. It was comforting. It smelled like James and for a moment or two, her family was reunited and complete.

Nora walked towards the wall where Shelly, her great aunt, was again being preserved within the mysterious liquid. Almost dead looking, it broke Nora's heart. She stared into the lifeless eyes before her. They were milky white.

'Oh shelly, my friends are in desperate need of a boost. If only your gift was passed down to me, I could have foreseen this and helped everyone escape Merryville in time. But, even then we would have died from the burns that plagued the rest of the planet. We couldn't have won either way,' she said. Nora thought she saw Shelly move slightly in her preservation liquid. She wondered if her mind was playing tricks on her, she wanted something good to happen so much her mind is messing with her. 'Please Shelly, if you can hear me, tell us what to do,' she added.

There was a movement in the tank, Nora knew she wasn't imagining it. Her great aunt raised her hand to the glass, slowly and smoothly, as if she was a robot on a pre-set routine. Nora raised her hand in the same manner to the same position.

There was a heat running through her arm and

up to her head, it was burning, though she did not want to move her hand away. If there was a way to help the others she wanted to help, still the heat grew hotter. Nora was sure that her hand was blistering on the glass.

A few moments passed, the temperature still rising, then there seemed to be a bolt of electricity, it struck like lightning all around her arm it travelled, great white sparks moving towards her head. Still she kept her hand in place. The sound the light made sounded like pure electrical currents.

Nora was propelled backwards by an almighty blast of electrical energy, it sent her through the air. Sharon, Jane and George saw and Sharon screamed at the sight. The light source in the room flickered and a loud buzz sound was produced. A power surge.

Their oldest friend hit the floor with a bang. Immediately the others surrounded her, held her hands. George supported her head, there was blood which coated his hands. He knew that she was bleeding heavily, he could feel it. His fingers were slippery.

'Oh my god, oh my. What do we do? Are you ok Nora?' Sharon panicked, though Nora seemed so calm and collected.

'I can see it all now dears. Blistrix has built something. It looks like a series of tunnels-' she broke off to catch her breath which was husky and sounded like she was reaching her end. 'The tunnels are behind the walls. He has a secret lair which all these passageways lead,' she looked at all of them individually, with so much love in her eyes.

'What shall we do about you though?' Jane asked.

'Don't worry about me, Jane. Any of you. I asked for a sign… to help us…this was it… I'm dying,' she said calmly and collected.

'No you're not. I'm scared Jane,' Sharon trembled. Jane just looked at Sharon with reassuring eyes and pulled focus back on Nora who was looking towards Sharon.

'Don't be scared dear, I'm not scared,' she announced. 'Make sure that you all catch that evil creature.'

Sharon, George and Jane all had tears in their eyes which wondered down their faces, to their chins and hung there for a moment before dripping to the floor.

'We will not let you down Mrs. White,' George explained.

'I *know* you won't,' a smiled played across her face. 'You're a good man,' she winked a cheeky wink, then closed her eyes. 'I will see you all again one day,' she added, then with a large, final breath, she was gone.

ENTITY: THE COMPLETE TRILOGY!

*

<u>TechSPACE Written Transmission #19</u>

We are finding it hard to continue with our daily jobs, the food supply has run out and our water supply will soon become nonexistent. Also, to make matters worse, our H20 filter does not work, so we cannot even recycle urine into water. I keep wondering to myself why I am still writing these notes, but it would be something to look back on if we get out of this alive. Though I am skeptical that that will ever happen. I am trying to stay brave for the others, but I'm obviously not a convincing actor.

Please, again, if you can hear us. We need help. We need saving.

Regards,

Mark Noir
Research Team Captain

Chapter 9

'If what you are saying is true, then…' Izazon stopped and looked at all who were present in the room. 'There is no telling where he could be. I will instruct my army to continue to search. Jane, George and Sharon, you are no longer safe here in The Chamber. We need to think of something else,' Izazon finished then turned to his council and spoke their mysterious and intriguing dialect.

'We told our friend Nora, we would fight and find Blistrix. We are going on the search too,' Sharon said, stepping forward. George and Jane followed her lead and stepped forward also. The three of them united, despite the bitter taste of loss and isolation they all felt. Jane and George realised that there was nothing else to lose, they wanted to honor Nora's last wish and fight for the closure and justice they all craved. One reason was for Nora, but also for James, Alex, Mark as well as all the others they had lost along the way. All the millions of people that perished at the hands of Blistrix.

They all felt so much hatred for the runaway Ocularit, Blistrix. All three of the survivors lost their friends and family when the light came down to earth and opened up a new, dark chapter in history. Further loss had been felt since being aboard the ship and they needed to finish the job they were now in tasked with.

Sharon felt confident that they could now do their mission, especially in light of the revelation Nora had told them. It at least gave a little insight into where Blistrix and Luvax may be hiding... or planning their next move.

Izazon looked at them all, their spirit and urge to carry on inspired him and touched him deep down. He felt emotions he had never felt before.

'That is the meaning of true courage. I would like to object to your ideas of joining my people on the search, but...' he stopped and turned again to his council, then back again when interrupted by Sharon.

'But?' Sharon said.

'After everything you humans have been through since our worlds collided, you carry on. Please, follow me to the armory. We need to have more protection if you are to be a part of my army,' Izazon announced, whilst leading the humans from the room and down the corridor outside.

The Optical room shone its lime green light as

they approached it. Izazon halted outside the room they were told never to enter when they arrived on board the vessel. A combination of beeps sounded and then the door opened, revealing a small room.

'Right, here we are,' he pointed to a few hard vests and shields, the survivors did not hesitate. They put on the armor, quick time.

An Ocularit rushed into the Optical room and conversed with Izazon in their own language. The humans all looked on as if they knew what they were talking about, but they did not have a clue. They looked upon Izazon and noticed that his emotions changed. Though he had only a large eyeball for a face it had a look of shock, fear and anxiousness within it. The Ocularit left the room and the space fell silent. Izazon did not speak for a while, then he turned to the humans.

'Well? Is everything ok?' Jane asked, still puffy eyed from the day's exhausting events.

'They have found a door. A secret door that is not on any blueprints for the ship,' he explained.

'That's good though isn't it? At least we are getting closer,' George said. 'We can finally find that monster and give him what he deserves.'

'Indeed, whatever is in these tunnels, please be careful and on guard at all times. There have been enough lives lost for one day…' he paused. It felt like he did not want the humans to find Blistrix at all. 'Right, follow me. I will take you to the entrance.'

Chapter 10

The room was dark and damp. There was a trickling sound coming from an unknown source. The walls looked almost sticky to the touch. The smell was that of rust and there was another smell in the air. It smelled sickly and could probably make a grown man breakdown and cry.

Blistrix turned to face his second in command, Luvax. Luvax could feel the unhappy eye that was staring at him from the other side of the room.

'What is wrong master?' Luvax asked, already shaking with fear. He knew that he was not happy and Luvax did not want to make his master angry. He had seen what Blistrix was capable of and didn't fancy getting on the wrong side of him.

'You have disposed of the weakest link, you needed to go for the father. Taking that infant man is going to make those other beast stronger. Do you not think? By taking away the life they have created they will not care about what happens to themselves now. They have lost everything and they will fight with brutal strength. You fool,' he explained then turned, so he did not have to look at Luvax. He could feel his blood boil.

'I- I'm sorry master,' Luvax said sounding sincere, though he was worried it may already be too late.

'You will be. Go now and do the job properly this time,' he dismissed Luvax, who scurried from the room just as quick as his limbs would take him.

'As for me,' Blistrix said to the now empty room. 'I've got to unleash my own trick. They will not believe what is coming for them.' He could not help but laugh, which echoed in the space and chased Luvax further down the dark, gloomy corridors.

*

'These tunnels could go on for miles for all we know. There could be hundreds of rooms. This ship is big enough without making it twice as big with the hidden areas,' Izazon said to the humans.

'I'll give it to your son, he knows how to plan,' Jane said, sounding hopeless. She wondered if they would ever finish the mission. Would they be able to stop Blistrix and whoever else he's got in his army? She felt, as well as George, that the death of the two Ocularits would bring some closure to James' death so they all felt like they needed to try.

'Well, we have lost too much to give up now. We must soldier on. My army is exploring the tunnels. I think that you three should rest for a while. Get some refreshments and recharge your energy. Tomorrow is going to be busy,' Izazon explained. All the humans were tired and the thought of a drink sounded like bliss in a hostile, isolated desert. They all slumped to the floor and all surrendered to exhaustion and slept. They slept a sleep so deep, there were no dreams.

*

'Awake,' Blistrix shouted as he pressed a button on his display panel. The room remained dark though a sound was heard from the other side of the gloomy room, then there were footsteps. A figure stepped into a single, bright ray of light, which emanated above the ceiling from a higher level.

'Ahhh, James my servant, you do look good after your upgrade,' Blistrix said then laughed his evil laugh. He looked in awe of his marvelous creation. 'It has been a mess around here. I need something I can depend on.'

James Peterson's likeness now emerged into the light. It looked just like him in the face. His body was that of a giant machine, it had wires and tubes connecting electrical charges making the robot able to move just like a human.

'Now. Let's begin. This is going to be brilliant. I'm going to have some fun with you.'

*

TechSPACE Written Transmission #20

We are becoming weak. All we seem to do now is sleep. We do not even have the energy to talk to each other, though there is nothing more to talk about now. Nadia had the last of the water supply today and so now we are more desperate than we have been before. Even writing these transmissions is taking so much energy. The view from our craft has not changed much we cannot see anything that we recognise so we have no idea how far away we are.

I feel like a broken record when I say, please help us. I can imagine we are too far away to get through now. We are still floating into unknown space…it all looks the same. If someone is still reading this, please tell our families that we love them.

Regards,

Mark Noir
Research Team Captain

Chapter 11

Sleep subsided for the survivors. All three that remained opened their eyes slowly and just laid there looking at the walls. There was no movement, all of them knew that the day had come for them to fight and bring justice to all who they have lost. It was up to them and them alone to do it. The task at hand was heavy on all their hearts. They wanted so much to succeed.

All George and Jane could think about was their little boy, who had been snatched and killed by the monster that was holding all the cards. Both felt so much anger towards Blistrix, they had to bring themselves some closure to all that had happened. George thought back to the night of the BBQ, the night everything changed. It was a nice night and there was so much laughter and such a good atmosphere... then it was gone in a matter of seconds. The light came down and then their fight for life began. He could not believe how far they had come since then. He could not believe that living in space would be something that he had gotten used to. *How is this normal?* He asked himself, still staring blankly at the cold wall in front of him.

Jane had a similar thought running through her mind. She also began thinking back to *that* night. She almost felt euphoric and high on life that night, then it all changed so quickly. She recalled how fast the people were fleeing from their home and suddenly it was quiet and depressing. Jane turned around and held George for a second or two, she felt like she could breakdown at the drop of a hat, but knew that she needed to fight and stay strong. *This is going to be a hard day,* she thought to herself.

Izazon walked into the room after all their brains were back up and running for the events which lay ahead.

'So, are we ready for this?' he asked. His eye looked bloodshot almost, as if from crying or lack of sleep. Jane knew why, Blistrix was his son and the thought that he is so hated must be killing him on the inside. She put herself in his shoes and wondered what she would do. She thought that she would probably cry as well.

Sharon stood up first, followed by the Petersons. They all donned their protective clothing and then stepped forward towards Izazon who then walked out of the room and signaled them to follow him to the entrance of the tunnels.

'Remember what I told you last time. Be on guard and expect anything. We have no idea what plans he may have in store for us. Also remember to use your stun guns to shoot him in his eye. Good Luck,' Izazon said, walking with his eye faced down towards the floor. Then there was silence as they walked through empty, dark rooms and long corridors to the tunnel.

*

'Master, they are coming. They have found our secret corridors,' Luvax said to Blistrix, who was still admiring his robot James Peterson.

'I know. I saw them on the camera. It is no worry to me. They will be greeted by this,' He said revealing his creation to Luvax, who was taken back at the sight of the marvelous machine.

'What is it?'

'This is our winning move. As you couldn't dispose of the father. I am going to use this creation to lure him into a false sense of security and then…well, I'll leave the next part to your own imagination. He will die at his sons hands,' he said whilst laughing his most sinister laugh yet. It made even Luvax shudder with fright.

'Why do you want to fight, master?' Luvax asked and then there was instant silence from Blistrix who looked towards him with his menacing eye.

'How dare you question me,' the creature said whilst turning on the switch to activate the robot. The robot stood up and walked towards Luvax. A rotating saw protruded from the machines body and Luvax knew that he had said the wrong thing. As the machine got ever closer to Luvax, Blistrix's laughter grew, until in the room there was only him and his machine.

*

They arrived at the tunnels entrance and were wary about going in. The tunnel was pitch black there was a musty smell that emanated from it. George stepped in first and was immediately aware of how cold it felt. Following George was Jane and then Sharon. They all walked in a conga line into the dark unknown, bracing themselves for everything that might happen.

Izazon watched as the final three humans in existence walked into what could be their last day alive.

Chapter 12

The tunnel seemed to go on forever. There was no light at all. The three remaining humans could just about see each other's outlines, they were left with their own imaginations. They were holding each other in a line formation walking into whatever was waiting for them. At times their eyes would think there was light up ahead, but only seconds later they realised they were just hoping for it so they continued.

George was in front. He had no clue where he was supposed to be going. He felt the wall to find his way. The wall was icy and damp. He had no idea what was on the walls and he did not want to find out, they had a sticky texture to them. He walked the line slowly so they wouldn't hit into any obstacles. Behind him, holding onto his shoulder was Jane, who was feeling anxious about what might be waiting for them in the tunnels. Behind her was Sharon, who felt the same way, though she was sweating with fear, but feeling so cold she shook.

There was a sound of pipes dripping and air escaping cylinders all around them. There was a slight draft which brought the smell of rotting flesh, blood and rust. Without the lights to guide them, they felt as if the walls were closing in on them. Wires and pipes hung down from the ceiling, making them all jump whenever one brushed past them. They knew they were in the bowels of the ship and that anything was possible. All of them were in uncharted territory. The feeling of being alone and vulnerable were dominant. Still the tunnel continued…

It felt like a long time, eventually they reached a corner and turned to continue down another corridor. All wondered how long this would go on for.

'Where are we going?' Sharon asked, breaking the silence making the other two jump slightly.

'I have no idea, I'm just feeling my way along. Who knows how long these tunnels go on for,' George replied. Jane stayed silent, her heart still beating from the surprise of Sharon's question. 'We just need to carry on walking and hope that we get some light soon.'

They continued again in silence, their footsteps echoing throughout the space behind and ahead of them.

*

Blistrix watched on the unsuspecting humans, listened to every word and footstep they made. He moved around his barely lit lair, thinking about his next move and when to execute it. He felt an overwhelming sense of joy at how far his plans had come.

'It's time,' he said to his Jamesbot. The robot understood the request and then set about getting to work.

*

'Did you hear that?' George asked. The others remained quiet. 'It sounded like…' he stopped and listened to something the others could not hear. 'It sounds like James.' As he said this Jane's heart leapt in her chest and the joy she felt all of a sudden overshadowed everything else. She suddenly felt some hope that James was still alive and ok, waiting for them to come and rescue him.

'We must be close, remember how sly and cunning Blistrix can be,' Sharon said, reminding them that everything may not be as it seemed.

'It is definitely him Jane. I can hear him getting louder,' George said, then Jane and Sharon heard something also. It did sound like James. They moved along the corridor quicker than before, unable to wait to see their son once again.

'Daddy... he is here,' the voice said. The words echoed mysteriously.

'Something isn't right here. George, he never called you daddy. Be careful,' Jane said. She then realised that what Sharon said might be what is happening. She felt that Blistrix is luring them into a trap, but there was something in her that needed to see and be sure.

'Daddy... he is hurting me,' the voice made tears come to Jane's eyes, it sounded just like James and the pictures she saw in her head were terrifying. George carried on, determined to find the source of the voice, whether it was James or not.

'...he knows you are coming... he knows everything...'

Sharon was becoming ever more scared with every step that they took. To her it felt like they were in a scene from a horror movie. They were the stupid people that investigate and get killed.

'Guys, I really think that we should find another direction to go in. This is going to end badly,' Sharon said to the Petersons.

'There is nowhere else to go. We need to carry on. I know you are scared, we all are,' Jane said.

'You're all going to die here...' the voice said, more sinister with every word it said. But they were

determined to find whatever was speaking. The joy Jane felt earlier had diminished and now rose curiosity and fear as well as a range of other unlikable emotions. They all stayed quiet and kept moving forward.

'You're getting closer... please go back... it's what he wants,' the voice stated.

Footsteps still echoed down the endless corridors and passageways. There seemed to be a little light up ahead of them so they aimed towards it. They slowed down slightly as their eyes were slowly becoming aware of their surroundings.

'At last, a little light. Maybe we can find out what the hell is going on,' George said. The ladies remained quiet and followed George's lead.

'You're silly to go any further. Get ready to face what you seek...' the voice said as the humans turned another corner into a big open space.

*

<u>TechSPACE Written Transmission #22</u>

I cannot believe that we are still finding ways to survive. It amazes me how long the human body can go on. We have resorted to less conventional ways to get our vitamins and instead of water, finding other things to keep us hydrated, I won't go into details. Our location is still unknown, we have not seen anything different for a while. I'm sure we are still moving though, I can feel some vibration from the surrounding area.

The rest of the team are preserving their energy and taking naps. Vincent has tried to fix the H2o purifier with no success. I thought I would just write this quick note down before I get some rest also.

Regards,

Mark Noir
Research Team Captain

Chapter 13

Izazon waited anxiously for any news of the survivors and of his son, Blistrix. He paced the length of his private quarters, worrying and thinking about the different outcomes. With silence pulsing, his mind was able to work into overdrive, making himself crazy with all the pictures that presented themselves. He hoped that the humans succeed, though he did not want any harm to come to Blistrix, his only son. He knew that Blistrix had made so many problems, but at the end of all that, he was still his father. Izazon was stuck in the middle. He felt that whatever the outcome, he would be devastated.

A member of his council came into the room after a while of thinking. He reported that there was no news on any situations. The High Emperor thanked the council member and dismissed him from his quarters. Izazon continued with his thinking. He knew what he would have to do with whatever outcome happened. He had some plans,

plans that would help or hinder his race and position as Emperor of the Ocularit people.

*

'Can you see anything George?' Jane asked. They all looked around the seemingly empty room waiting in anticipation.

'Not yet,' he replied. They all felt like they were being watched, though they could not find the source of this feeling. There were a lot of dark corners within the large space.

The walls were dripping with some sort of sticky looking liquid. The liquid dropped to the floor with regular timing. The air was cold and the smell of rotting flesh was still prominent. They could see the many pipes and wires hanging from the ceiling, every now and again a puff of air could be seen escaping from them, making them jump.

'Where do we go now?' Sharon asked. She spotted a few passageways in which they could explore, though she did not want to go down any of the paths. She was still shaking with fear and the feeling of anxiousness was to the maximum. Her hands were clammy with sweat.

'I – I don't know,' George said. He also looked at the variety of paths he could choose. 'I'm torn between them all. Who knows where they all lead.'

Jane stood next to George, looking around at their surroundings. There was nothing she could say to help sway the decision. She, like Sharon did not want to go down any of them. George moved towards one of the opening and the other two followed.

There was a sudden noise which pierced through their heads. It was high pitched, like a dog whistle for humans. The noise halted, but the ringing in their ears continued. There was a bang, then another, something was coming their way. They stepped back to the centre of the room, where they had stood moments before. The banging noises continued to get louder.

The lights went out with a mighty blast.

Frozen still, they could not have prepared themselves for what was standing in front of them when the light returned.

*

Izazon still resided in his quarters when the lights fell. It was short lived as the backup system kicked in and the emergency lights turned on, though they were dim and gloomy. The light described what he was feeling, lifeless and drained of energy. The council member from before rushed in.

'What is going on?' Izazon asked, bracing

himself for bad news.

'There was a power surge that stemmed from the bowels of the ship. We believe the humans may have found him, sir,' the council member said. Izazon did not react to this. In his mind he knew that this was what he was anxious about and now that it was here he did not know what to do.

'Thank you for informing me. There is still a lot of work to do. Let's just hope no one suffers too much. Please return to your station and let me know the minute you hear anything,' he said to his council member, who obeyed and left Izazon in isolation, alone with his thoughts.

Chapter 14

As the lights reignited, there was an uneasy feeling of being watched by someone... or something. They all felt the same presence. It was like a weight on their shoulders, they were scared for what might present itself.

The Jamesbot, in all its glory, stood into the light which dully shone down on the depressing situation. It took the survivors by surprise and it shocked Jane and George to their cores. The face of the thing that stood in front of them looked exactly like that of their late son. The robot was huge. The face was connected to many wires and metal components which span and moved with every step it took. Jane stumbled back, nearly losing her balance as tears rolled down her eyes. She almost wanted to love the robot with James' face but knew that this was not a friend, but a foe. Both she and George had a deep anger towards the monster Blistrix, for making them face the machine which stood in front of them. The robot had long arms which had some sort of device attached to both limbs. It reminded George of robot movies he used to watch as a kid.

'What do you want?' Sharon asked, as she knew the other two were in shock about what was standing in front of them. There was no reply from the machine, it turned its head towards Sharon and then resumed its position, still and silent, staring into space.

'Welcome all,' a voice came from an unknown place, it was him, Blistrix. *'This is my little creation. I call it the Jamesbot... He is harmless, to me anyway. But I'm afraid the road ends here.'*

Jane, George and Sharon all stood like statues whilst Blistrix said what he had to say. Nothing was said in response. It was just quiet, all that could be heard was the occasional tick or scrap from the machine's engine.

'Jamesbot... Activate sequence one,' Blistrix said. Almost immediately after, the Jamesbot launched into movement. It stomped over to George who was then struck down by one of its large heavy arms. George let out a scream of pain, his blood was soon visible, pooling on the floor.

'George,' Jane screamed. Sharon tried to stay strong, though she felt helpless. Her body did not want to move, it was frozen.

The robot proceeded closer to George, who was

recoiling on the floor from the pain. It continued with his command and hit George again with another almighty blow. Again the screams of pain escaped from George. Then it went silent, George was still on the floor. Sharon readied her stun gun and fired, there was no effect to the robot. Again she fired, still nothing happened. Jane pulled a pipe from a nearby wall and rammed it into the neck of the machine, causing it to shut down.

'George, oh George. Speak to me,' Jane said, kneeling by his side. 'I will not lose you too.' It remained silent for a moment, then George let out a husky breath, Jane felt such relief. Sharon had tears rolling down her cheek which dripped onto the floor.

'HA. You think it's that easy do you? Jamesbot...initiate sequence two. Finish them.' Blistrix commanded the robot and the eyes of the machine lit up a bright green. The robot stood up again and continued to target George. Jane and Sharon both grabbed what they could to defeat the beast of metal. The Jamesbot's arm turned red and the device at the end of the arm sparked and then a flame was produced. The heat was so intense that Sharon, Jane and George, who was still laying in pain on the floor, looked away from it.

The robot looked towards George, who managed to look back and then the flame was fully activated. Sharon and Jane continued to beat the robot, finally making it stop and fall to the floor. Though they did not stop hitting at the machine. They managed to disconnect a leg and an arm. The green lights in its eyes stopped shining. It was defeated, but the trio was now a duo.

Jane walked towards the body of George, which was burned. Bone was protruding from the flesh and she just knelt down by his side and sobbed. She felt like she could not go on. She had lost her son and her husband. What was there left to fight for. She thought about just giving up, she looked towards Sharon who was also crying at George's side. Both hugged each other to try and give what comfort they had left. Jane could not take her eyes off the charred body laying before her, through the grotesque look did not extinguish Jane's love for George.

'Well that was disappointing. Only one kill. What was it like to see your offspring kill your beloved?' Blistrix asked. Jane and Sharon, in an instant felt so much rage and anger sprang again.

'I'll kill you… you…' Jane couldn't continue. She was so angry and so sad at the same time she could not catch her breath.

'Ooo promises, promises. You'll have to find me first,' he said and then laughed the way they had become accustomed too.

'Jane, we need to go,' Sharon said to her friend.

'I know.' She turned once more to look at George. She kissed his head, still scolding hot from the flames, then stood and walked side by side with Sharon into another hallway which was just as dark and mysterious as the first one they entered.

*

Izazon stared into space, wondering how the humans were getting on with their mission. He somehow wished that he could help them get back to their lives and make everything ok again. He sat up quickly and pondered an idea.

'Is it possible?' he muttered to himself in his language. He thought some more about what he could do and then walked from his quarters back towards the Chamber.

Chapter 15

Izazon entered the Chamber and looked around at the empty space, he began to feel so thoughtful about all that had happened up to this point. He felt ashamed that his offspring would bring so much destruction and pain to a planet and furthermore to the universe. He had destroyed families, a whole civilization, for what… revenge. Izazon knew it was a petty excuse for bloodshed. Though he was hurt by the fact that the human race caused their own planet to die, he would not of even thought about doing something so dastardly… so evil.

The High Emperor made his way over to the preserved body of Shelly White, who looked so peaceful in her unconscious like state. He observed the life that was there, knew that there was something special that this human could do. *Is there a way to make all this better again?* He thought to himself. He remained still, studying the body like a work of art. He was amazed that his son could create something that could preserve life this well.

He wondered what else he was capable of, good and bad.

The cold from space emanated from the walls as he stood there alone. He could feel his eye becoming more bloodshot, he felt exhausted. The past few hours and days had taken their toll on the aging emperor, as well as the others who were onboard the vessel.

'Tell me… Is there a way for all this to be good again?' He asked Shelly who remained unresponsive. He felt desperate, he wanted to make all that Blistrix had done right again. His father's instinct told him to cover his tracks, but the tracks seemed like they were too deep to fill. Uncharacteristically he slumped down onto the floor and began to show an emotion not fit of his people, he cried.

'Please, human, tell me a way,' he pleaded with Shelly again. There was a little movement within the tank. The motion made Izazon stand up and get himself together, there may be hope after all.

Shelly started to twitch.

*

'I can't see where we are going Jane,' Sharon said whilst walking slowly down the dark and depressing corridor.

'Me either. Just hold my hand and we will get through this,' Jane said back. The anger she felt towards Blistrix was second to none. Jane was worried of what she was capable of doing. Deep down, her gut did not care about what happened next. Her mind was all over the place, she could not concentrate and did not think of any consequences.

It wasn't long before they saw a little light up ahead of them.

'Head for the light Sharon. We will get this monster,' Jane said, feeling determined. 'For all he has done, he will pay.' The two woman readied their stun guns, preparing themselves for what could be coming up. Their surroundings, though horrid, became insignificant. Before long, they entered another room.

The room they had entered was full with machines, computer systems and screens all around. The screen showed all the areas of the vessel, so *he* could keep watch. Both Sharon and Jane had never seen so many wires and technology in one place, some machines were completely beyond them. The walls remained their sticky and gloomy looking selves. Though the chrome and metal of the equipment looked so clean and modern that it looked completely out of place.

'Where are you?' Jane shouted, though there was no reply. Something fell over in the distance, making them both jump. They felt their hearts beat faster. Sharon was sure she would have a heart attack at any moment. Jane tried to stay cool. She knew she had to finish this once and for all.

'Come out you coward,' Jane called again, though this time a laugh echoed around the room and down the many corridors. Sharon looked around wondering where it had come from, though neither women could pin point it.

Both of them started looking around the room more and then they stumbled across pictures of earth and Blistrix plans to destroy the planet. She looked through the pictures, remembering some of the places that had been a big part of their lives. Some of the pictures were old, showing the Merryville Asylum where Shelly had been taken too. A loud bang brought them both back to the present and they looked around quickly, but nothing was there.

'We know you are here,' Sharon said. The room suddenly felt much cooler and the hairs on the back of their neck stood to attention.

'Welcome to my lair,' Blistrix said, showing himself within the room. Jane and Sharon, stepped back away from him and studied him. They wondered if he had any more tricks up his sleeve. Though he admitted that it was just him and that he did not need any more help to finish them.

TechSPACE Written Transmission #26

I don't know if it's just because I'm exhausted and becoming dehydrated, but I have been getting the feeling that we are being watched lately. There seems to be an odd presence. The universe outside our ship looks the same, so why am I feeling this way. Maybe I'm being paranoid, I'm starting to lose my head.

The rest of the crew are barely hanging on, I fear that within a few more days, lives will be lost. I wish I believed in miracles because we need one right about now. Never before have I felt so helpless and hopeless in equal measures. I hope I live to document another day.

Regards,

Mark Noir
Research Team Captain

Chapter 16

'What do you want from us, you monster?' Jane screamed at the specimen of evil that was standing before her. He looked at the humans with his solo eye, darting from Jane to Sharon. His body language came across as confident and they were scared about how he was going to finish them.

'I am going to finish what I set out to do. You puny human scum are the vilest creations that ever existed. Your people have killed more Ocularits than stars in the universe,' he replied. The room went suddenly cold, Jane and Sharon did not say anything else. Both of them did not know what to do, so they just stood there like statues, staring.

'Are you ready?' Blistrix asked the two ladies.

'For what?' Sharon asked back.

'You know. Your times have come,' he answered with a smugness in his voice. The dim light which filled the room suddenly turned black and the luxury of sight was taken away from the final two survivors. Blistrix was laughing, though it sounded like he was all around them, in front, behind and above.

Jane braced herself for whatever might happen, she was waiting with her eyes tightly closed. She wondered which direction he would attack from.

Sharon thought similar thoughts, though her mind was thinking about Alex, he is what kept her safe and she wanted to think of him in her final moments.

The long time ago neighbors held hands, ready and waiting. They both had their hands on their stun guns ready to shoot at the first chance they got.

Then he attacked.

*

Shelly pointed to a lever. Izazon walked towards it and took a deep breath before pulling it down. As he did this, the water levels began to drop, just as it had done when Blistrix revealed her to the humans for the first time.

As the water level lowered, there was a change in Shelly's skin colour. It started to look more *real*, more human. Izazon was watching every moment, anticipating what she had to say to him. The wires that penetrated her skin changed colour, again just like the first time and then before he knew it, Izazon was standing in front of a perfectly preserved human specimen.

'Shelly. My name is Izazon. My...' Izazon managed before Shelly interrupted him.

'I know who you are. I know all, it is a gift,' she looked thoughtful. '...though sometimes it feels more like a curse, a spell I have been put under. It is a cruel existence. It's more cruel that no one else knows how I am feeling, so apparently that makes me insane.'

'It must be horrid. You are unique and special, not only amongst humans, but so many more species of life that exist. I want you to tell me about my son.'

'Oh yes, Blistrix. He is an evil entity, though I am unsure about why he has chosen to be so bad. As you know he wasn't always like this, I can see it in the pictures in my brain. As a father it must be horrible for you to see him going down this dark route. He will not stop,' she warned. 'I remember when he came to visit me in the asylum the first couple of times, there was so much hate there. I could not believe the negative energy I felt emanating from him. But that is another story for another day,' she recalled.

'Tell me, is there any hope? Can I clear his name after these terrible acts that he has done?' Izazon asked, desperately wanted her to say yes.

'He is powerful, more powerful than you I'm

afraid, more powerful than most. I can visualise two outcomes… There may be hope yet.' Izazon looked at her with want and need for the knowledge she possessed.

'Please, tell me.'

*

The lights returned showing a scene of such bloody chaos. A slaughterhouse with blood and body parts splattered carelessly around the small room, which has left one human remaining. Standing in a pool of blood which sloshed as she found her stance and balance again.

'Now then, do you have any last requests?' Blistrix asked the remaining human. She looked at him, her face dry, tears which should be there, dried up from the loss she has previously suffered.

'Just one thing…go die you evil creature.'

*

<u>TechSPACE Written Transmission #28</u>

```
We are still struggling through. I
feel like there is nothing else to
tell. The mission has long since
finished and the hope of returning
home has long since died.
```

It sounds mad, I want to die out here now. If I cannot return home then I want to die. I know that I have a family back on earth to live and fight through for, but there is no fight left in me. I feel so weak, so depressed with every thought that crosses my mind. As this team's captain, I feel like I need to be strong, that is why I have resulted in writing my true feelings down in these transmissions. It is the only thing that is keeping me sane up here in the cold, dark depths of space.

Regards,

Mark Noir
Research Team Captain

Chapter 17

'I have one request. Though it can only be fulfilled by me. I want to finish you forever. You have caused so much pain to me and my friends and family,' the lone survivor said.

'There is nothing that can stop me now,' Blistrix laughed his laugh, it shook the floor which she stood on. She steadied her stun gun and pointed it at the beast which was circling her like a lion would its prey. His footsteps on the metal floor clicked and clacked as he moved.

'I don't want to live, though I want you to die more. I want you to pay for what you have done. I want some closure before I leave this life as well. I cannot go on with all that has happened. For all I know I am the last human in the universe left.'

'Maybe you are. Maybe you're not. Remember there is the old lady I have in the preservation fluid. She is not only a human, but one of the best from your species. She is the only one I could have liked. She could see *all*.'

'You still tried to kill her… in the end.'

'I did, my mind just can't shake the rage I feel for humans and what they did to my people. My sister, Xion, was disfigured from the fallout of our planet. I promised her I would make Earth pay for what happened. Your planet was so toxic, so polluted, it was us that suffered.'

'Revenge does not get anyone anywhere. Haven't you figured that out? If you do end up killing me, the other Ocularits know what you have done. There is no turning back.'

'They can be bought back round, they *will* trust me again,' he said with such surety in his voice. His eye never left her, she felt like she should look away, even just for a second. Though she knew that he was unpredictable and she didn't want to risk it.

'What was your sister like?' she asked trying to approach him from a different angle.

'She was amazing, my father took it hard when she died, he was just as angry as I was, though he has always had the power to forgive. But I can't, her eye was slanted and there was no colour in it. She stared at me with her milk coloured dreamy eye, it still haunts me now. I remember the day that it happened like it was yesterday. Many of us Ocularits were on a mission away from the safety of our planet. When we returned there was so much destruction, it looked like we had been away for years. The whole planet was burned and Ocularits were dead everywhere. We wondered ourselves what had happened, then I saw Xion. She was a leading scientist in our community, she knew exactly what had happened. The pollution from your dirty planet leaked from your broken O-Zone layer and hit our fragile, sterile planet and boom, it was all over. You infected our planet like an untreatable disease, it's like our planet was a clean surface and was smudged by a dirty finger, never to be the same,' he stopped, then his posture changed. He knew what the human was trying to do. 'Let's not dwell on the past. Only one of us is going to be leaving this place alive. The other will be taken to the mortuary awaiting disposal.'

Blistrix lunged swiftly towards her, but she was prepared and jumped from his grasp. Then he repeated, so did she.

'Not so stupid,' he said to her, he chuckled again which sounded just as sinister as the first time he did it. The survivor stayed vacant faced, monitoring his every move, ready to dodge whatever he might do next.

The Ocularit jumped to the ceiling, as he did he grabbed the fixture which hung down and managed to crawl above. He then dropped down and landed on her. Stunned, she did not have enough time or speed to move. He was now in the driving seat.

*

'Remember what I said Izazon, this task relies on your complete commitment and total loss. It will be difficult, but it might just save the planet,' Shelly explained to Izazon, who was now sat distraught from the revelations she told him.

'I must do it. I must make things right,' He said to himself more than to Shelly. 'You must of known what I would say, I don't know why I need to tell you all this,' he continued.

'I don't know everything, though I seem to see the future, everything can be changed. Nothing is set in stone.'

The room went deadly quiet whilst Izazon contemplated his decision. He rested his hands on the sides of his eye, the way a human might hold their head in their hands.

'There is one thing I know for sure… I know you will make the right decision,' Shelly's voice went husky all of a sudden. Her skin aged before the high emperor's eye, turning flakey and then all the life left her body. She was gone, just like that. The preservation liquid dried up and there was no way to revive her. A tear rolled down his eye and dropped down onto the floor with a little splashing sound.

*

'Well, it looks like you are in a tight spot,' Blistrix said to the last of the human race.

'It might seem that way,' she pulled the trigger of the stun gun which launched Blistrix from her body and across the room. Her fingers burned from the close impact shot. Though the pain never seemed to register because the anger was coursing through her body. She never thought that she could hate something more than she hated *him*.

Walking over to where Blistrix laid, his eye was closed, she walked gingerly towards the seemingly lifeless body. She knew that she must be crazy to investigate his body, though she had to make sure the job was done. The human knelt down beside him and everything seemed more quiet than usual, there was a buzzing in her ears.

His eye opened quickly, making her jump back.

She shot.

He was finished. He convulsed and a blue coloured liquid leaked from his eye. She was more than happy with what she had done and did not regret a thing. He had taken everything from her, she was ready to face the high emperor. Then she wanted to leave this life and be with her husband and son. She wanted to see their faces again, even just for a second.

*

TechSPACE Written Transmission #31

Mark wanted me to write todays transmission. I don't know why he keeps on with these diaries, there is no chance to get back to Earth now. I know he knows this, but I sometimes think that he is delusional to the fact.

So here goes the transmission. We are all weak, Mark has managed to catch something and is in bed...sick. Vincent, Matt and Thomas are not much better, they are trying to gather some molded food for our dinner. They have found a few things that have been mushed in our storage cupboard. That's all I have to write for now, there is nothing left to document.

Nadia Trott
Research Team, Second in Command

Chapter 18

Jane's walk back to the entrance of the tunnel seemed like a long, lonely trek. At times she thought that she must have taken a wrong turn, then was put back on path by the trail of destruction which had been caused. The tunnels which had held so many revelations and challenges for them to overcome, now quiet and haunting. There was the occasional dripping of a pipe somewhere in the distance which echoed around the labyrinth of corridors, every time making Jane jump and almost recoil down on the floor.

She could see a light at the end of the dark, gloomy tunnel. Her eyes had trouble adjusting to the brightness of the "normal" corridors. The white light hugged her and welcomed her back to some sort of safety. She was welcomed by a few Ocularits who were in the army fleet. Jane looked both left and right and saw no sign of Izazon. He was the only one she wanted.

'Where is he?' She asked the Ocularit closest to

her. 'I need to tell him,' she added. He pointed her in the right direction with a long finger, once they would of scared her, now a part of her life.

The last remaining human walked down the short corridor, walking past the Ocular room with the lime green light emanated from the door, then stopped just outside The Chamber. She did not know why she was so scared to face Izazon, after all he told them to do it. She was just about to push the door open then lost her nerve, her mind thought back to their time on board the ship, how scared they all were when they started and what become of them. Her mind thought further back to the day the light came down and destroyed all that was human and "normal". Though what happened before then seemed so far away, it was difficult to pull a memory from the brain.

She wasn't sure how long she had been thinking for, her eyes started to get tired from the events she had attended. She turned and pushed the door open, revealing Izazon standing at the far end of the room with a limp Shelly White slumped next to him. She walked cautiously over to him, for the sight she beheld did not look like it was.

'What happened?' she asked the aging emperor, with a slight anger in her voice.

'I had a conversation with this magnificent specimen. She told me all. For the first time in my life my eye is truly open,' he said looking at her through a barrier of tears. The air went cold, though Jane didn't feel any threat. She knew that Shelly had a gift, that she would be fair and non-judgmental towards Izazon and his people.

'She was a very wise woman. Just like her great, great niece, Nora. I wish I made more of an effort with her. I was always brushing her off. I feel like such a cow,' Jane said thinking back to the last conversation she had with Nora on Earth.

Jane sat next to Izazon and reluctantly put her arm around his neck.

'I did the job, though I am the only one left. He killed George and Sharon,' she explained to him, she said it with no tone in her voice… it was like she was immune to the heartache and pain that was being inflicted on her. It was not a nice thing to get used to but still it had happened. She felt so strong and yet so weak at the same time.

'You have been a brave soul. I would have staked my life that you would be the last one standing. You had it in you from the start, even though you did not know it. Sometimes in life we get used to a routine and the thought of doing something different is scary. Without James and George by your side you had no alternative but to do it yourself.'

Jane felt a bit confused about what he was

saying, she was sure that some of the words were what he wanted to hear.

'I will send one of my people to retrieve the body of Blistrix and bring him here.'

*

Sometime went by and Jane was worried that Blistrix wasn't really dead and had escaped to another secret location. The thought of her loss being for nothing made her feel sick, she could feel her stomach acid rising in her throat, like she would vomit at any moment.

'Why aren't they here yet?' She asked Izazon, who was preparing a table for his son to lay on.

'Do not worry, I told the army to check out all the other rooms whilst they were there, check for any more of my people who may have joined the other side.'

Jane paced the room and her footsteps echoed around the room. So she just waiting some more.

...

Finally the doors to The Chamber opened and three Ocularits brought in the body of Blistrix. His eye had now lost its colour, Jane imagined that's what his sister had looked like after the humans destroyed their planet. It brought a tear to Jane's eye as she looked upon the culprit of such pain caused.

The Ocularits placed him on the table in front of Izazon who looked upon it. His eye looked away, Jane walked around the table to meet him.

'Are you ok?' She asked.

'The love you are supposed to feel towards an offspring is not what I am feeling now?' he said. 'As his father of course I do love him, but it's a different kind of love. I love him because I have to, not because I want to.'

'I know. It must be difficult.'

'What he has done to your friends and family is unforgivable, let alone what he has done to your planet. I want to make it up to you. I'm sure there is nothing else you want more than to see your family again,' he said and turned back towards the lifeless body laying before him. 'I will repay his debts.'

Chapter 19

Jane looked at him confused. Izazon looked down at the body of his deceased son. He was tampering with some wires and connecting them to clamps.

'Are you stupid? My family and friends are dead, thanks to that *monster*,' she said angrily.

'There was a reason why I didn't want you to kill Blistrix, only stun him,' he said whilst continuing to connect wires to clamps. He was connecting these clamps to the hands and feet of Blistrix.

'What are you going on about?' Jane asked, still feeling a bit angry. Half her mind was beginning to hope again, but she denied herself to get too excited.

'Do you want to see them again or not?'

'Well of course, more than anything in the universe. I'm still confused. Is there a way? Is there a way to make all this go away.'

Izazon looked upon the last survivor with a worried look in his eye, Jane could feel it.

'Indeed there is. I wasn't one hundred percent sure that there was a way until I spoke with Shelly. There was always something in the back of my mind that told me not to kill Blistrix,' he said, the words sounded mournful and final. He finished connecting the wires to Blistrix then walked across the room to a lone chair and slumped down hard upon it.

'Can you do it? Here? Now?' She had so many questions. She felt like she would burst. 'I want to see my family again... I want to have my friends back,' Jane had a tear roll down her eyes, it was one of a joy, excitement and worry in equal measures. Desperation filled her and the thought that things could go back to normal again seemed too good to be true.

'We can. Right now...' he stumbled on his words. 'To do so I must sacrifice my son. I know he is a villain, an evil traitor. But, like I said I am still his father and there is love there,' he stopped talking and looked down towards the floor.

Jane knew all too well the feeling of loss, only if it has been for a short while, the wounds internally are fresh. Immediately, she was able to put herself in his shoes and knew that if it was her she couldn't do it.

'Myself and Shelly spoke about this at length. There is nothing else to say really. I have made a commitment to myself that I am going to do this. I need to make all his wrongdoings right again.'

He stood up and walked again over towards the body of Blistrix. Jane walked closely behind. She was still a bit confused and was worried about what it might take to make it all better again. There was still going to be a loss, not everyone will be happy. Though, Jane wanted to see James and George again, she felt like she would do anything.

'When I press this button it will all be over. I needed his body, his blood is concentrated evil and that's what the machine needs. The blood still needs to be pumping around the body for it to work, this is why I wanted you to only stun him.'

It was all starting to come together. Izazon made some final arrangements to the wires and the machine that it was connected to. The machine looked like nothing more than a drip they would give to someone in a hospital bed.

'Are you ready?' He asked Jane, though he already knew the answer. Jane simply nodded at him. 'Good. This won't hurt much but after it's done all will be forgotten. You will be happy again. The half of our ship that was buried under your town will go back and lay dormant till the end of time,' he explained this to Jane, who couldn't hear as she was anticipating the next step. Izazon looked down at Blistrix. 'Goodbye son.'

He pressed a switch on the machine and there was a rumble noise. It grew louder and then it stopped suddenly. A great blue bolt of light came down from the ceiling, it hit Blistrix's body. Little blue lights protruded from his body, like bolts of electricity. This continued for only a few minutes. Jane looked up towards Izazon who was watching the lights fly around the room. It got brighter and brighter.

'Thank you,' Jane mouthed to Izazon, who just nodded. The light grew brighter and brighter. Blue electric bolts still flashed, not slowing but intensifying.

Brighter…

Blue was fading to white.

Brighter…

Jane blacked out. Then there was silence. Then a ringing in her ears. It was painful, though she did not cry out.

*

A breeze on her shoulder…

*

TechSPACE Written Transmission #35

ENTITY: THE COMPLETE TRILOGY!

Just when I thought all was lost we have been rescued by a ship. It is carrying us with them, I assume for an embarkation process.

The ship looks a bit strange though, like a giant eye ball, a bit freaky. Though, it can't get any worse… can it?

Regards,

Mark Noir
Research Team Captain

Chapter 20

The smell of the BBQ filled the air.

Jane felt dazed and dizzy but soon she regained her focus.

'Burgers ready,' called George from the grill. As he said that the people stopped what they were doing and swarmed around the BBQ like flies around a light. This happened at all parties and George learnt to just stand back and let people fight over how well done they liked their burgers.

'You would of thought that they had never eaten before, ha,' George chuckled, walking towards where Jane was standing, looking out over the hills. 'Jane, are you ok?' he asked her.

'Ye- Yeah. Yes. Sorry, I must have been daydreaming about something,' she looked out at the marvelous view before her.

'Was it something nice you were dreaming about?' He asked.

'I- I can't remember. Never mind, look at that view. Wonderful night isn't it George.'

'Amazing, absolutely amazing,' he confirmed and looked around. 'Where is James, has he escaped the pleasures of listening to Nora go on about how she changed his nappies as a baby,' He said and they laughed in unison.

'Probably, lucky boy. Just leave him, he will be down when he is hungry,' Jane said.

The sun was nearly out of view and the summer night was creeping in. The sky was free from clouds and other obstructions, apart from a few sparkling stars which hung in the air. The breeze was still warm but cooling down more and more by the second. The sky was bright pink, but now changing to a dark purple colour. The smell of freshly cooked burgers was everywhere they turned their heads. The birds which were chirping earlier had now nested for the night and the owl occasionally hooted its song. In the distance the sound of crickets were audible, a beautiful sunset fell over the English town which was, absolutely stunning on the backdrop of hills, all different shades of greens, like a patchwork quilt. The seemingly endless space which surrounded the Petersons home, made them all feel so free.

'Well, the sausages won't cook themselves,' said George.

'Ok, honey. I'll be over in a moment, this scene is just too amazing to walk away from,' she said. He kissed her on the cheek and resumed his position behind the grill. Jane just basked in the glory of the transition from day into night. The sky gradually became darker by the second, which gave way to more amazing colours, purples and blues. It brought a tear to her eye, which slowly trickled down her cheek, a happy tear. As she cast her eyes across the sky, she caught sight of a twinkling star in the distance shining bright, brighter than any other star before. Jane turned to face the party again and walked back to join the rest of the party guests.

'Look at that star up there,' she said to Sharon and Alex Jones.

'Which one? They are all the same,' Sharon asked. Jane looked around and the bright star she had seen only a moment ago had disappeared.

'Never mind. Enjoy the party, I'll see you again later,' Jane said then continued mingling with the other party guests. She had a nice chat with the Robinstons about Mr. Robinstons promotion and a chat to Nora about a party she wanted to host. Jane didn't really want to go, but something in her mind told her to go, so she reluctantly agreed.

*

The party was over and Jane and George were finishing their drinks on the garden swing which looked out over the beautiful landscape which surrounded them.

'Well I think that party was a success,' George said once he finished his last mouthful.

'It was perfect. I think it's time for bed, I'm getting tired,' she agreed and they both stood up and walked into the house. Jane locked the patio door, as she did so, she saw a rabbit in the distance hopping further and further out of view.

The rabbit hopped down the garden and into the surrounding field. It hopped and hopped towards the town line. Its ear twitched, it could hear something, something only an animal could hear. It followed the noise, but discovered nothing.

What it didn't know was, below the ground was a beeper going off, there was a vessel that had missed its chance to connect to its component.

So the beeping continued, hoping to one day reconnect with its mothership.

Reconnect to a distant entity.

The End!

Afterword

It feels like a lifetime ago that I created this world and characters. They all still hold a special place in my heart.

After many start and stops, I decided to compile all three Entity volumes into this one book as a sort of rebrand. Many things have changed in my life both physically and mentally and a completely new start is what was eventually called for.

THE COVER

Way back when, before the creation of the Entity books I wanted to have a cover which was real life. An edited photograph. I even went as far as to take the pictures and upload them onto my Facebook page as early promotional material. Due to lack of both knowledge and programming know how, this idea was eventually scrapped, much to my dismay.

The covers of Entity 1,2 and 3, were created by me as a bit of a consolation cover. It was what I could manage at that moment with the time, money and resources I had. Although happy with them at the time, my enjoyment from the covers diminished over time. It did not convey the image I had intended.

Fast forward to now. I have slightly more understanding of how things work. I have enlisted the help of a friend in *Ashley's Photography* whom agreed to help me.

I explained my original dream of the cover which I thought was lost. He was able to create a cover that I had envisioned all those years ago, long before the story of Entity was on paper.

Ashley's Photography can be found on Facebook where his work can be admired and purchased.

WHAT'S NEXT?

Now this re-release is completed and in the public eye, I'm going to be looking at other stories not only within the Entity universe but completely new stories. Ideas have been building in the years since I first released these books. I think it's about time people were let into my mind, if even for an hour or so.

Follow me on Facebook at M. Purkiss for all updates!

Printed in Great Britain
by Amazon